SKATE

ALSO AVAILABLE FROM LAUREL-LEAF BOOKS

WHALE TALK, *Chris Crutcher*

I AM THE CHEESE, *Robert Cormier*

THE CHOCOLATE WAR, *Robert Cormier*

ACCELERATION, *Graham McNamee*

NORMAN TUTTLE ON THE LAST FRONTIER
Tom Bodett

THE LAST SNAKE RUNNER
Kimberley Griffiths Little

TEX, *S. E. Hinton*

WRESTLING STURBRIDGE, *Rich Wallace*

MICHAEL HARMON

LAUREL-LEAF
BOOKS

Published by Laurel-Leaf
an imprint of Random House Children's Books
a division of Random House, Inc.
New York

This is a work of fiction. Names, characters, places, and incidents either
are the product of the author's imagination or are used fictitiously.
Any resemblance to actual persons, living or dead, events, or locales
is entirely coincidental.

Published in hardcover in the United States by Alfred A. Knopf Books for
Young Readers, an imprint of Random House Children's Books, a division
of Random House, Inc., New York, in 2006. This edition published by
arrangement with Alfred A. Knopf Books for Young Readers.

Laurel-Leaf and colophon are registered trademarks of Random House, Inc.

www.randomhouse.com/teens

Educators and librarians, for a variety of teaching tools, visit us at
www.randomhouse.com/teachers

RL: 6.2

ISBN: 978-0-553-49510-2

February 2008

Printed in the United States of America

10 9 8 7 6 5 4

First Laurel-Leaf Edition

For
Sydney and Dylan

SKATE

Chapter One

*T*ony Freemont can't keep his mouth shut for longer than thirty seconds at a time because Tony is one of those guys where words come out in uncontrollable spasms. He looked at the cut of my ex-girlfriend's bra through her gym shirt, and I could almost feel it coming.

"Dude, gotta be Victoria's Secret," he said, bending his head to my ear. Coach Schmidt's eyes flicked our way, a big fist wrapped around a small blue paddle, but the Ping-Pong sermon continued.

I had no desire to talk to Tony Freemont about the cut of Veronica Jorgenson's bra, because I'd seen that particular one without the shirt on over it, and even though we're not together anymore and it burns a bit, my mouth stays shut about those things. Tony knows I still like her, too, and every chance he gets, he rubs it in.

Tony is a linebacker for Morrison High's junior varsity football team, and Veronica is captain of the JV cheerleaders. He's had a thing for her since we started school, and that she dated a guy, even for a little while, with four earrings and another in his eyebrow had him questioning the all-American qualities a Morrison High jacket bestowed upon a person unlike myself.

He nodded her way. "Skater boy wipes it again. Take a look at what you're missing, dorko."

I kept my eyes on Coach to avoid the push-ups I knew were coming if we got caught, but I almost couldn't resist body-slamming him into the floor. Now wasn't the time to teach Tony a lesson in manners, and anyway, I'd have half the JV defensive line after me if I did. "I heard your mom sticks a cork up your ass to shut you up, Tony. Did it come out?"

That closed his mouth for a few seconds, but it was too late. Coach zeroed in on us with those steel pop rivets for eyes and fell silent. Coach Schmidt is a two-hundred-thirty-pound stump of flesh with a head sticking out of the top of it, and aside from having to shave more than me, she's the first, and only, female football coach the city of Spokane has ever had. She's also the state women's arm-wrestling champion four years running. Her eyes slid from us to Veronica, then back, as if she knew exactly what we were talking about. Just like Mom but with big biceps. "Did you boys have something to share with us today?"

"No, ma'am." I smiled because she was posed like a state arm-wrestling champion in a ballet class; the paddle midswing, her beefy arms frozen like an action figure. I was tempted to give the class an explanation of Tony's preoccupation with Veronica's boob-holders, but I didn't. Coach Schmidt doesn't like anything funny unless it has to do with cartilage damage, dislocated shoulders, or death on the playing field, and I'm already on her bad side for blowing off the sports program my freshman year.

She stared at me, then assumed a non–Ping-Pong stance

before shooting daggers at Tony. He's the mouth, so I figured I'd slide by. "And you, Mr. Freemont?" she said. "Do you have something *enlightening* to say?"

"No, ma'am."

She pointed to the ground. "Push-ups."

I bent to hit the floor, and Tony held up his arm, smiling. "Bad shoulder. Coach Thompson says I should take it easy for a few days. Strained it on the press."

Coach Thompson is the JV football coach, so it looked like Tony had an out. Play a sport at Morrison, you got an out. Some way, somehow, it's always different if you wear a jacket. On the other hand, if you wear ripped black cargos, Anarchy shirts, and secondhand Converse tennis shoes and pack a skateboard, you're a social leper walking around with enough open sores to have every teacher grimacing like they have a bad rash. Coach Schmidt gave him a skeptical look. "See a doctor?"

He shook his head. "Just a strain."

"Excused," she said, letting him skate, then pointed to me. "Hit it, McDermott."

Coach Schmidt believes the key to life is push-ups. It's been rumored she once ordered the Coke machine in the cafeteria to pull down fifty for spitting out the wrong soda. Rumor also has it that the machine did them. She also believes the answer to every question in the universe is contained in motivational sports anecdotes. She pointed again to the lacquered wood floor when I didn't hit it fast enough.

I started pushing up. Instead of going on with her instruction, she made the class wait for me to expend myself. Besides a bunch of Ping-Pong tables and a blue-paddle-holding gym teacher who looks like she could squat a semi-truck, there wasn't much to look

3

at, so the class looked at me. That's the way Schmidt liked it, because her philosophy includes the idea that being bathed in the fire of public humiliation makes for stronger character.

Tony looked at everything but me as I tried not to embarrass myself any more than I had already, knowing what was running through my head but not stupid enough to say anything, either. The only thing strained on his big galoof body was his brain for thinking so quickly.

I felt sorry for myself while I did my push-ups, thinking about how convenient things seemed to be for students who play sports at this school. The gem of the city, Morrison *is* sports. College scouts come every year digging for talent, and the pedestal of sportsdom is the biggest buffer a kid can have against getting in trouble on campus. I did forty-six and couldn't do any more, so I collapsed on the floor, staring at her feet. Even her ankles had muscles.

"More," she growled, trying to bring out the disgraced competitor in me. "Come on, McDermott, reach deep and you'll find it."

My arms were wet noodles, and the only thing I could find by digging deep was a word Coach Schmidt would find offensive. "No," I said.

She bent down, her fists on her knees. Coach Schmidt had a one-track mind, and that track is for everybody, whether they like it or not. A minor bump in the road and everything's cool, but once you get on her list, she's like a marine drill sergeant. She'll bust your nuts until there's nothing left or she'll kill you in the process. I'm in the middle of a yearlong hell week. "How about three days' detention?"

I stood. "Fine."

She pointed to the door of her office. "Wait."

I walked past the protective wire mesh on the window and stood at the door. Coach Schmidt instructed the class, then ordered everybody to choose a table. A minute later, she stomped my way, her thigh muscles flexing. She unlocked the door, opened it with one hand, and grabbed my arm with the other, leading me into the office.

There are five things a state arm-wrestling champion has to have to win four years in a row, and they were on my arm right then. Her fingers were like steel sausage pincers, and I yanked away, a knee-jerk reaction, sending her fist into the doorjamb as she lost her grip. Instant alarm popped into her eyes, and I felt her guard go up before she settled into a simmering stare. "Sit down." I sat in the chair in front of her desk and she sat, too. "Why do you pull this on me, Ian?"

"I didn't pull anything. And don't grab me again." Ping-Pong paddling echoed outside, and my arms ached. I thought of Tony, who was probably looking at Veronica's butt right now while he nursed his strained shoulder.

"It's your attitude, Ian." She folded her hands on the desk, letting me see her arms. Everything about her was power and control and competition. "And," she added, "I'm the one who gives the orders around here, not you, and I don't need to remind you that there is zero tolerance"—she made an O with her finger and thumb—"for violence at this school."

I was surprised she said it, and also surprised I'd seen that alarm flash in her eyes when I jerked away from her hand. Like she'd been scared for a minute. "Don't grab me again, and you won't have to worry about it."

She glowered. "Don't test me, Ian."

"I'm not testing you, Miss Schmidt," I said.

"Coach Schmidt," she corrected.

I didn't answer.

"I know what you're thinking, and it's not true."

"What's not true?"

She rolled her eyes. "That the only reason Tony Freemont didn't hit the deck with you is because he's a player."

Coach Schmidt's term for anybody at Morrison who played sports is a *player*. Everybody else was a student. "You know as well as I do that he doesn't have a strained anything."

"I don't know that."

"Then why was he shooting hoops with Mark Fitz and Cory Bernard before class? Not too good for a star linebacker's strained shoulder," I said.

She raised her eyebrows. "I didn't know that."

I laughed. "Yes, you did."

Her brow lowered. "Are you calling me a liar, Mr. McDermott?"

I smiled. "So it's Mr. McDermott now." I shook my head. "Call yourself what you want. You gave him permission to open the ball cage. I watched you do it."

"Ian," she said, more conciliatory now. "Tony Freemont has nothing to do with why you're in here. He's not the issue. *You* are the issue. Nobody else can or should take responsibility for your attitude, and I think I've given you more than enough chances to prove yourself."

"I didn't know I had to prove anything."

"Life is a proving ground."

I shook my head again. "I'm not running for this school." The last thing in the world I wanted was to wear Morrison's colors. Even if a part of me wanted to run, and even if I knew I could whip anybody on the track.

"You have talent."

"But it's only worth something if I look a certain way, right?"

She clenched her jaw. "We've had this conversation before, Ian. Morrison High has standards for leadership, and if you play a sport here, you're a leader. You'll find that anywhere you go, and it's fair." She looked me up and down. "I know your 'image' is important to you, but we have standards."

At the beginning of my freshman year, I beat out the school's senior mile-runner during the routine fitness test everybody has to take. Coach Schmidt saw me do it, and the next day the track coach, Mr. Florence, called me into his office with an offer. Get rid of the punked hair and earrings, and I'd have a spot. No tryouts. I'd skate onto the team, and that'd be it. I declined, and things went downhill from there, with Coach Florence telling me straight out that Morrison High didn't have use for kids with no motivation.

If there was one thing worse than a nonplayer, it was a nonplayer who passed on an opportunity to join the elite. Coach Schmidt saw another record on the books when she looked at me, and to deny what she saw as my duty to the school was akin to putting a dagger through the king's eye. Coach Florence couldn't even look at me without sneering, and he made my life a living hell every chance he got.

I didn't buy the leadership spiel. "You're just pissed because I won't be one of the special kids."

She shook her head. "I'm 'pissed' because you are passing up an opportunity to better yourself, Ian. Being rebellious doesn't get you anything in this life. It gets you down and out, and I don't want to see that happen to you."

"You want a title."

She nodded. "I do. I'm proud of this school and proud of the players who work for it. There's nothing wrong with that."

"Except that there's over a thousand other people around here you don't care about."

She tucked a longer piece of her short hair behind her ear. "That's not true."

"I suppose that's why Coach Florence busts my nuts every chance he gets and why Tony Freemont slides out of push-ups?" I looked at her. "What if I told you I strained my shoulder skating? I'd be standing next to him and you'd be stuck with your thumb up your butt in front of the whole class? Hardly."

Coach sat back in her chair, steepling her fingers on her midsection and trying to hold her patience. "I like you, Ian."

"You don't know me."

"I like your spirit."

"Bull."

She raised her eyebrows. "Well, maybe you and I can come to some sort of agreement."

"What agreement?"

"You respect me, I respect you. That's all."

"Maybe you should tell it to that prick Florence."

She shook her head. "I can't listen to that, Ian."

"You can't listen to a lot of things, can you?"

Coach Schmidt took a breath, held it, then sighed. "You're on a road that's going nowhere, Ian. That's why I'm trying here."

I looked her up and down. "Trying to what? Get it through my head that the only thing Morrison High School is interested in is itself?" I laughed. "You prove that one every day, *Coach*. No thanks."

She frowned, and I knew I'd gone too far. "Get out."

Chapter Two

Morrison High is a sprawling, open campus, with its buildings forming a haphazard perimeter around a central courtyard. Fifteen hundred students hustle from the arts building to the music building, across the yard to the cafeteria, on to the administration offices, and finally to the two-story Goliath of the main academic center.

Inlaid in the middle of the brick-paved courtyard is the pride of the school: the Morrison High Vikings coat of arms. Every freshman is told in no uncertain terms that if a student is seen stepping on the tiled emblem as they hustle to class, God himself will blast down past a screen of archangels, run a quick fishhook, and drive a pigskin torpedo through their head. Fire and brimstone be damned, it's the hallowed and speeding football that'll get you every time, and needless to say, I step on it every chance I get.

Next to the emblem and set on a concrete pedestal is the school bell, which the principal, Mr. Spence, rang the morning after every sports victory, banging away at the thing like a camel hair–robed monk celebrating a new itch.

9

Every day after gym, I met Bennie Campbell near the bell and we walked to math class together. Bennie Campbell is a genius disguised as a runt-bodied skater punk with a homosexual for a father and enough dysfunction in his life to warrant his mother leaving the state and not wanting to have anything to do with either of them ever again. He's also not afraid to tell anybody anything, and that's why I like him.

While I waited for him, I noticed the bell was balanced on its swivel upside down again. That would be Bennie's handiwork, and I knew what was inside. "You peed in it again, didn't you?" I said as he angled his way over to me.

Bennie's front teeth have a gap big enough to fire torpedoes from, and he's got freckles, a small, fine-boned face, big hands and feet, short arms, long legs, and no butt. Nothing really fits together with him, but he can skate like a pro. We'd been friends for seven years. He showed his teeth through a grin as big as a horse's and pointed to the bell. "That? Oh, yeah, I guess I did. Had an urge last night." He looked around. "We won yesterday. Yippee."

"I suppose you having an urge and us winning are pure coincidence."

He shrugged, distracted by the bell. "He should be coming out any sec. Let's wait."

I nodded, knowing we'd be late for math but feeling a twinge of evil curiosity. "I can't believe he never gets it. It's not like it rained last night or something."

He looked at me like I was crazy. "Who ever said you have to be smart to run the show?"

Just then, Mr. Spence came out of the administration building and walked purposefully toward the bell, waving and saying hello to various students. Bennie giggled. "A buck for me if he dumps

10

it toward him, a buck for you if it's away," he said, watching Spence prepare for the ringing.

As usual, Mr. Spence stared at the emblem for a moment, the adoration on his face reminding me of Moses and his stone tablets, then turned his eyes to the bell. The Urine Bell, as Bennie called it.

"Here goes," Bennie said.

The pedestal is high enough so that only Shaq would be able to see if there was anything in the bell, and Bennie had peed in it a few times, so I figured the odds were even both ways for the bet. Mr. Spence raised his arm to the rim of the upside-down bell and, without any hesitation, pulled it toward him. A good pint of pee splashed over the waist-high pedestal and ran down to the emblem, its grout lines filling with Bennie's urine.

Before he could jump away, a few droplets bled dark on Mr. Spence's thighs, and Bennie giggled under his breath. "Dumb is as dumb does. Let's go. That ringing drives me up a wall."

As Bennie and I hustled up the stairs to math, I saw Veronica out of the corner of my eye and thought about Tony's words of wisdom and what I was missing under that shirt. I don't care, though. Not much, anyway. I know why she dated me, and it had much more to do with her father than with me.

"I heard the man-masher got you today," Bennie said.

We walked down the hall, which was thin with late students and thick with silence. "Push-ups."

"Dyke."

"You don't know she's gay, Bennie."

"Well, I know she's a bitch. Is that good enough for you?"

"Just because your dad is gay doesn't mean you have the okay to do that, Bennie."

His laugh echoed down the near empty hall. "Fag, queer,

11

dyke, lesbo, whatever. You know I'm fine with my dad being a homo. At least on the outside."

"Other people don't know that. They just hear you bag on people all the time."

"And other people look at me like I'm a freak because my dad likes guys. Go sing to them, choirboy."

It was true, but it wasn't the half of it. The teasing started easily enough when Ben's dad had come out of the closet the year before, and Spokane is like a huge rumor mill in the first place. A lady who worked with Ben's dad had a son going to Morrison High, and the word got out, gaining steam, especially because Bennie's dad was so open with it.

With the cat out of the bag and Bennie being Bennie, from then on he used every chance he got to throw other people's homophobia in their faces, but I'd never heard him use the term *gay*. He was a walking irony. One minute he'd call his dad a fag, and the next he'd blast into somebody for being homophobic, calling them everything in the book that people who stand up for gay people shouldn't.

It was always *fag* or *queer* or *pole smoker* or something else that would have any other kid hanging from the administration building's flagpole for bigoted speech, which wasn't allowed on school grounds. And while he got away with it with the teachers, the students were a different story.

Within the first three months of our freshman year, he was known around campus as the fag's son, and half the football team started calling him Fagson. For most of the guys, it was just another way to give a kid who didn't fit in a hard time, but for a few, it went beyond that.

A varsity linebacker named Jeff Stearns was one of them, and he tormented Bennie every chance he got. It ended one day in the school parking lot. He pounded Ben, broke his nose, and put him down for the count.

I'm bigger than most fifteen-year-olds and stronger than the average schmo, built like a distance runner, long legs and arms, but my shoulders are wide and I've worked out enough to give me some decent guns. I suppose good genes is one of the few things I can thank my long-gone father for. I'd always assumed he was an athlete of some kind.

Jeff Stearns was a mountain of a linebacker, and I knew one thing: it wouldn't end for Ben unless somebody ended it for him. I caught up to Jeff the next day, just him and me near the equipment shed at the football field, and told him to lay off Bennie. We ended up beating the living crap out of each other, but when it all came down to it and I stood over him waiting for the next round, he smiled through busted and bloody lips, nodded, and told me I was all right. I'm not all right with him, but the football team leaves Bennie alone now.

There's a light blue water tower half a mile from where I sat in Mr. Kuvocek's math class, and I stared at it every day. After a stern look at us for being late, Mr. Kuvocek continued his lesson as we took our seats. Kuvocek's class was a no-brainer, and I'd taken it for no other reasons than less homework and easy tests. Less homework because I didn't have time for it, and easy tests so I could pass without too much trouble. Mr. Kuvocek looked at me like just another punker with spiked hair and no brain, so he pretty much left me to staring out the window.

On the top level of the main building, Mr. Kuvocek's class

13

looks out past the tan diamond of the baseball field, the rubber-matted oval of the running track, three field houses, and an overgrown field where the beginnings of another housing development rise from the weeds. Past that and on a little farther is the tower.

As I looked, a man in a harness hung down the side of the tower. He had half of the words I LOVE KIM painted over with blue and was working his way over for the rest. I'd watched him for two days now, and it looked as if the job would be done by the end of the day, but I knew he'd be back up there soon. The tower is Morrison High's alternative billboard. I wondered who Kim was and wondered more about the idiot who risked his neck painting three-foot-high block letters on it for her, but I liked the idea.

Chapter Three

I'm out every day at two-thirty, and my little brother, Sammy, is out at three. He's in fourth grade, ten years old, and his school is ten blocks away from Morrison High. Five blocks in between is Glasgow's Mini-Mart, and it's there that most of my after-school grocery shopping is done.

Mr. Glasgow stood behind the counter when I brought up my stuff. I put a box of Tuna Helper, a can of tuna, and a Mountain Dew on the counter, and he grunted a hello. Mr. Glasgow is a Russian immigrant, and even though I'd stood across the counter from him countless times, he acts like he's never seen me before. He punched buttons on the cash register, the bell rang, and he turned the lit-green total amount so I could see it, pointing with a thick finger.

Two dollars twenty-five cents for the Helper, ninety-nine cents for the tuna, and a dollar seven for the Mountain Dew left me nearly broke, but we had dinner, and Sammy would love me for the Dew. Mr. Glasgow, like he did every time I came in, nodded, smiled, looked at the board in my hand, and pointed to the NO SKATEBOARDING sign on the door. Skaters are the scourge of modern civilization. I stuffed the shopping bag in my pack, put it on, and waited until I was on the sidewalk to skate.

Thirty seconds after the bell rang at Sammy's school, he busted down the stairs with a flood of kids, his backpack flying behind him and his board tucked under his arm. Parents and children milled around, kids did somersaults down the grass embankment to the sidewalk, and one of his teachers, Mrs. Jenkins, waved to me from the steps. I told Sammy to stay where he was and made my way to her.

"Hello, Ian," she said.

"Hi, Mrs. Jenkins," I said. Sammy was slow—not retarded, though—and he spent part of his day in the Developmentally Impaired classroom to help him keep up. Mrs. Jenkins had him the other part of the day. With the "normal" kids.

She stood on the stairs three steps above me and studied my face. "Sammy didn't hand in his homework again, Ian."

I looked back at Sammy, then at Mrs. Jenkins. "He did it. Maybe he left it at home. How'd he do on the test?"

She frowned as if she was thinking about something sad and shook her head. "Not well, Ian."

I could tell she liked Sam, but he was hard to work with. It's like half the time he can't concentrate for longer than five seconds. "We studied."

"You know, Ian, he's a good boy, and he's been responding to direction better." She put her hand on the rail. "You also know he's been seeing the counselor, Mr. Franken?"

I nodded. He'd been in a fight two weeks ago, and they'd stuck him in counseling two days a week for anger management and conflict resolution. They'd sent a note home explaining to Mom that he needed to learn to deal nonviolently with "spats" on the playground. I'd signed it and sent it back the next day, not bothering to ask what happened to the kid who'd pestered him.

She paused. "Mr. Franken has tried to contact your mother, but . . ."

"She's busy a lot of the time," I said. "I'll tell her to call you."

"I would appreciate that," she said, then said goodbye.

I returned to Sammy, and we wound our way through chatting mothers and screaming kids, setting our boards down just past the last crossing guard. The only thing the same between Sammy and me was our eyes. Other than that, he was thick-boned and stocky and had chub under his chin, while I didn't have an extra ounce of fat on me. He walked pigeon-toed and didn't have a sense of the space he occupied, always bumping into people and tripping over himself. Walking next to him was like being in a bumper-car race, and it drove me crazy. Unless he was on a board. The kid was all grace when it came to that. "How'd you do on the test?"

"D."

"We studied, Sam. Come on. What happened?" I stopped.

He shrugged. "I tried. Big deal. I can't do it like you, anyway," he said. We'd studied for his grammar test three nights in a row. "It don't matter anyway, Ian."

"Doesn't," I corrected.

"Doesn't." He shrugged. "It *doesn't* matter anyway."

"You want to stay in fourth grade forever?"

"No."

"Then . . ." We'd had this conversation before.

"Then whatever. I'm dumb." He flipped his board up, caught it, and took a swig of Mountain Dew. "Thanks for the pop. What're we having for dinner?"

17

"Tuna stuff. We have some mayo left in the fridge."

"I'm sick of that."

"Eat dirt, then." I'm not a culinary master, but I have every boxed-casserole dish at the store down pat.

"Why can't we have hamburgers and fries?"

"Got any money?"

"No."

"Then shut up." A few blocks later, we skated past McDonald's, and Sammy reminded me of a starving African kid looking at a bowl of dung soup. I checked for drool on his chin and ruffled his hair. "If I can pick up a job, maybe we can have burgers this weekend."

Sammy hopped an empty bottle on his board, the clack of the wheels hitting pavement echoing from the brick wall next to us. "When's Mom gonna come home?"

"I don't know."

"She's been gone a long time. Did she call yet? She usually calls."

"They disconnected the phone again. And you know she'll come home."

Sammy shrugged. "Why don't she come home now? I want her home. Kyle says his mom is home *every* night. Why can't she be home every night? Then we could do stuff."

"She'll be home soon. How 'bout I show you a new grind on the boards? Bennie told me about an awesome rail downtown. We can check it out."

Sammy shrugged, determined to bug the hell out of me about Mom. "Maybe she'll be back when we get home, huh? She fixes tuna better than you."

We skated the last block to the house, skirting sections of

sidewalk thrust up like tents by maple tree roots underneath the concrete, and walked up the porch. Our house, faded paint peeling and loose boards creaking with every step, sat four doors in from the corner. To say we had a lawn was like saying the vacant lot across the street was a resort area. The only thing resorting in the lot were occasional bums, and the only things green in our yard were at least a thousand dandelions sprouting through the matted dead grass like sentinels on the lookout for intruders. The place reminded me of a big plate of hash browns sprinkled with parsley.

Mrs. Vander, our next-door neighbor and the person I least liked talking to, stood in her own yard, a complex landscape of flowers and bushes and manicured lawn, watering her ferns.

Sammy kick-flipped his board up the steps to the porch and slammed open the screen door, fumbling with the key around his neck before busting inside. I heard him yelling for Mom as I came up the porch, and I felt Mrs. Vander's eighty-year-old eyeballs drilling holes into my back.

"Young man?"

I didn't turn because I knew exactly what would happen next. I stared off into the vacant lot, imagining Mrs. Vander in Minnesota or Alaska or Burma. Seven months ago, a guy four blocks away got shot in a bad drug deal. They found him dead the next morning, his body limned with frost, in the lot across the street. I saw them carry the body, zipped up in a body bag, to the ambulance, and I went over later to see the blood on the ground.

I hadn't seen Mrs. Vander out there complaining to the coroner and the detectives about dead bodies and drugs and all the other things that this neighborhood was full of, but she didn't let a chance pass to rail on me about the yard.

"Young man!"

I turned. "Hello, Mrs. Vander."

Mrs. Vander wore floral-print housedresses and watered her ferns all day. She shook her hose at me. "Young man, you just look right over on your porch, near the corner. Go on, look."

I did. Coiled like a rope was a length of hose with a brand-new rainbow sprinkler sitting on top. I looked back to her, and when I didn't say anything, she shook her hose again.

"I purchased those for you yesterday afternoon. With my hard-earned money, I did. Spent it on you. Now you don't have any excuse to not water your lawn, so I want you to put your time to good use with my charity and make that place look respectable. Like it used to, you hear? It's a shambles, it is."

She had a pinched look on her face. Hers was the first gift I'd ever received out of spite. I didn't even know when the last time was that the place looked decent, but what I did know is that it was a weed farm when we moved in three years ago, and nothing much had changed. I looked up and down the block, where seven or eight yards were in the same shape as ours. Several others were better, and one or two looked like Mrs. Vander's. A few more were nothing more than small junkyards. "Thank you, Mrs. Vander."

She shooed me off with the hose. "Now you be a good boy and get that thing going. I can even help you if you'd like."

"That's okay, ma'am. Really." I looked at the hose and sprinkler, and I would've liked to shove them down her throat, but I didn't because picking on old people is totally not cool in any way. I opened the screen door, and it banged shut behind me, the push-rod on it shot. If I did water the damn lawn, I'd have to mow it, and we didn't have a mower. I smiled, wondering if Mrs.

Vander's contempt for us would go as far as a new mower, weed and feed, a gas can, gas, and paying our water bill. I didn't think so.

Mom wasn't home, and Sammy wasn't in sight, so I walked through the living room, past Sammy's pack on the floor, and into the kitchen, where I set my own backpack on the table and found a clean glass for a drink. I ran the tap until it was cold and filled the glass, taking a gulp. "Sammy! Pick your crap up by the door." I heard him come from Mom's room, go to our room, then walk to the kitchen on his way to the back door. He had a rolled-up piece of construction paper in his hand. I turned the tap off and swigged the rest of the glass. "She's not out back, Sam. She never goes out there."

He opened the back door, peeking through the busted screen. "She might be."

"Doing what? Gardening? Hang up your pack and get your board out of the way. She's not here."

He ignored me, scuttling out back, then came in a second later. "You were right." He sighed. "Dang. I did a picture today."

I glanced at it. "Let me see." He started unrolling the paper but fumbled and it fell to the floor. I picked it up. Four stick figures stood in front of a yellow house. Green grass surrounded it, smoke came from the chimney, and there was a tree off to the side. Two of the figures, one shorter than the other, were holding skateboards. Us. Sammy always wanted to dress like me, and we wore matching outfits. Black. One of the figures had long hair. Mom. I pointed to the last one. "Who's this?"

"Our dad." He tapped the drawing. "See? His face looks like mine. Same eyes, right? I did a good job on the eyes, didn't I?" He took the picture from me, and I nodded. "Just like Mom always says, huh? Eyes like the color of a baby deer's, right? Your eyes, too."

I looked at it. "You've never even seen our dad."

"So what? I can draw whatever I want, and besides, maybe he'll come here one day an' I can show him this."

"You think so? Why do you think he's not here, Sam?"

He shrugged, glowering. "I can draw whatever I want, and you're a butthead."

"I know, Sam, and I know I'm the biggest butthead in the world, but there's no use wishing for something that won't happen. He's gone."

He looked at his picture, keeping his eyes from me. "Do you remember him?"

Our dad was the guy who skated when he couldn't take it anymore. He bagged out on us before Sammy was even born. "Yeah, I remember him."

"What was he like?"

I didn't like thinking about him. "We do have the same eyes."

"What else?"

"Nothing, really."

He screwed up his face suspiciously. He asked about our father enough to know I didn't like talking about it. "You sure?"

I shrugged. "I don't want to talk about it."

"Tell me."

"He didn't want us. That's the only thing you need to know."

Anger flushed his cheeks. "Not so. Mom said he left because he had to get another job. They couldn't be together because of that, so shut up."

"You shut up, Sam. I remember him—you don't." The fact of the matter was that I did remember things. Before he left, he was always gone, and by the time Mom got pregnant with Sam, when I was four, he wasn't even living with us. Since then,

22

we hadn't seen a shadow of him. Ten years, and I couldn't even picture his face in my mind. Just snatches of him every once in a while.

"Well, Mom says I look more like him than you do, so you're just jealous."

I knew I'd hurt his feelings, but it made me mad. "I'm not jealous, Sam. I just don't want you wishing for something that will hurt you. And hey, we can put your drawing on the fridge for when Mom gets home, huh? She'll like it."

"You don't like it."

"I think it's great. Really. You're a good artist."

"Mr. Parker says I am, too. He's the art guy."

"I know. And you are. So go get your homework out. Mrs. Jenkins said you didn't hand yours in today. What happened to it?"

He kicked the floor. "I dunno."

I walked from the kitchen and picked up his pack, opening it and riffling through the papers. Soccer-camp flyer. Lice warning notice. Early-dismissal notifications. Fund-raiser information. Book orders. Last night's homework. "It's right here, Sam!" I called to the kitchen. "Why didn't you hand it in?"

"I couldn't find it," he yelled back. "You said we'd skate now."

I stuffed the papers away in his pack and came back to the kitchen. "Hand it in tomorrow, 'kay?" I stuck the tuna box in the cupboard and gathered our laundry from the bathroom. Sammy scampered out, picking up his stuff by the door like I asked him. I put the laundry in the bag hanging on the back door and counted the change in my pocket. "Sam!"

"What?"

"Don't get your clothes dirty till we have money for the wash." Crap. I didn't have any clean underwear, and even though

Sammy would wear the same pair for a year straight, I couldn't. I grabbed a few pairs from the bag and filled the sink with water, adding a squirt of dishwashing liquid to the mix. Ten minutes and a whole lot of scrubbing later, I wrung them out and set them on the kitchen table to dry.

An hour later, after wrangling Sammy through his homework and studying for this week's spelling test, I called to him to grab his board and walked outside to set the damn sprinkler up. I could make the old lady happy for at least a day, and I couldn't get Sammy's picture out of my head. Green grass. When I came back in, I glanced at the refrigerator. Sam's picture had changed. He'd scribbled out one of the figures. Me.

We skated downtown. The financial center across from the bus station has the best rails for grinding, and I showed Sammy the one Bennie had told me about, which was behind three huge Dumpsters near a side alley. Twenty minutes into it, a security guard rounded the corner and walked toward us.

"You boys are going to have to leave the premises," he said. "We don't allow skating here."

I knew just about every security guard downtown, and most of them were cool. This guy was new. "No problem." I picked up my board. Security guards and skateboarding went together like gasoline and matches, and this was a daily occurrence.

As the security guard turned to go, Sammy dropped his board and ran the grind again. The guard turned around, drawing up his shoulders and pointing. "Off the board, kid. I just told you—no skating on the premises."

Sammy ignored him, doing a one-eighty and heading back to the rail.

The guard walked toward him.

"We're leaving," I piped up, then looked at Sammy. He

wouldn't meet my eyes, but kept skating. I walked toward him, and he skated around me. "Sam, come on. We can hit Riverside."

He kept skating, his jaw set. He avoided eye contact with the guard, ignoring him, too, and I knew trouble was coming.

The guard looked at me for something, then back at Sam. I could tell he wasn't pissed, just irritated. Pissed would come next. "Come on, guys, don't do this. Just get off the property, huh? I don't want to call the cops."

I reached out to grab Sam, but he ducked under me. The guard was there, and he tried, too, running a few steps and finally snagging Sam's shirt. Sam struggled, his eyes at his feet. "Get off me, fucker!"

"Sam, *come on!*" I cried, but he wouldn't quit.

The guard wrapped one arm around him and grabbed his radio with his other arm, telling whoever was at the other end to call the police. Sammy kicked back and caught the guy on the shin, and he let go, hopping around on one foot and cussing. He ran at Sammy and tackled him, yanking him to his feet and shaking him. "What's your problem, kid? All's you had to do is get off the property, and now you get busted." He grabbed Sammy's shoulders, his face inches from Sammy's. "What are you, stupid?"

"Don't arrest him, sir. We'll leave. I promise." I looked at him, pleading. "Come on, man, he's only ten. Give him a break." I stumbled through all the things I could think to get him off the hook, but the guard wasn't buying it.

He studied me for a minute, and Sammy was mute, a flat look in his eyes. Then he pushed Sammy away, nearly knocking him down. "Don't come back."

I took Sammy's arm and grabbed our boards. We walked around the block, my hand still around Sammy's arm. "Why'd you do that, Sam? Goddamnit."

He shrugged. "He can't tell me what to do, and you can't, either."

"Yes, he can, Sam. You know that." I looked at him. "How many times have we been chased off?"

"A lot."

"He could have arrested you."

He looked at me with his storm-cloud face and smirked. "So?"

"So we're done. No more skating."

Chapter Four

A wiry guy with big arms and a thick mullet snaking down his neck sat on the couch eating our dinner when we got home. He wore cowboy boots and had a tattoo of a snake winding down his right forearm, the head ending on the back of his hand. Mom sat next to him with a plate of half-eaten Tuna Helper in front of her. Sammy dropped his board and ran, tumbling into her arms and screeching that she was back. She kissed his head and leaned back, smiling and hugging him.

She looked like hell. Her hair, long and dark, was thinning and straggly, and she'd lost more weight. I stood there watching the guy eat our dinner and didn't know what to do. He paid us no mind and shoved a load of food in his mouth, keeping his eyes on the TV. Mom's eyes came to rest on me. "Hi, sweetie."

I walked to the kitchen and looked at the empty casserole dish, turned around, and walked back into the living room. "We don't have anything else."

Mom nudged Sammy from her lap, and I noticed her hands shaking. She brushed a piece of hair behind her ear, looking at her plate. "I'm sorry, honey . . . I didn't know."

I walked over to the coffee table. "He's eating Sammy's dinner." I reached for his plate, and he grabbed my wrist, still forking food in his mouth, his eyes switching from the fuzzy TV to me.

"Ian, please . . ." Mom's eyes flicked from the guy to me at a million miles an hour.

I held the plate, and he held my wrist, and my bones rubbed together until I thought they'd break. He remained silent, slowly chewing his food as he squeezed harder, his eyes riveted on mine. I watched the vein on his arm pulse and noticed it followed along the belly of the snake tattoo. "Sammy needs to eat."

Mom gave me a blank look, and I let go of the plate. The guy let go of my wrist, his eyes following me. "You'd best be careful how you behave around me, boy," he said, and there was a meanness in his voice that sent a chill up my spine. He turned to Mom. "You didn't say you had no kids."

Sammy looked to Mom, but she didn't look back. She looked at me, then her own plate, then back to me. "We haven't eaten for a while, honey. I didn't know this was your dinner."

I had seventy-four cents in my pocket. I took it out and showed it to her. "That's all I have."

She dug in her pocket, but her hand came out empty. She looked at the guy. "Can you give them a few bucks, Gary?"

He looked me up and down. "What, seventeen?"

"Fifteen."

He chewed Sammy's dinner. "Big kid. Think you're tough?" His mouth was a slit. "The time I was fifteen, I was bustin' knuckles on carburetors, making a living. Get your own damn money." He flung a finger at Sammy. "Now you, there. You need somethin' to eat. You just take your mother's. Mother's supposed to feed her babies. She don't need anything but what I give her anyway." He turned to Mom, chuckling. "Ain't that right?"

Sammy looked at her plate and took a step forward. Mom sat silent, looking at her lap. I shook my head at Sammy. "Come on, Sam." I picked up my board, and Sammy, thank God, didn't push it this time. We closed the door behind us.

Out on the sidewalk, Sam dropped his board. "I could have shared it with her, Ian. She woulda. We could've all shared it."

"We can get our own."

"That guy's a jerk."

"Just ignore him." I started walking.

Sammy followed on his board. "What are we doing?"

"Getting dinner." We rode down to the grocery store and bought a can of vegetable soup for sixty-nine cents. I didn't want to go back home, but we had to eat, and I wasn't about to bang the damn can on the curb to open it.

We took the long way home, Sammy all the while asking why we were going the long way, and I finally told him that the longer we were gone, the better the chances that Gary would be gone, too. He wasn't, though, and as I opened the can of soup in the kitchen, Snake-man lit a pipe, took a hit, then passed it to Mom.

I stirred the soup with the burner on high and heard him ask Sammy if he wanted a hit, before exhaling with a laugh.

"Dinner's ready, Sam!" I yelled. Sammy came in while I poured the soup, and I told him to get pillows and a couple blankets.

He scrunched up his face. "Aww, man."

"Just go get them, Sammy."

"I hate it there."

I clanked the spoons in the bowls before the soup boiled, snapping at him. "Just go, okay?" I stuffed a lighter in my back pocket and opened the back door while Sammy got the stuff. The shed was full of old paint cans and rusty tools, but I'd cleared a

29

space about a year ago, and it did just fine when Mom brought guys home.

Last year I'd found an old mattress behind the apartment building two blocks over and brought it home, and after I set our stuff next to it, I plunked down. "We're not going back in, so don't even ask." Sometimes the smoke got so thick I'd get high just breathing, and one of these days, Sammy *would* take a hit.

Sammy dropped the blankets, and I lit two utility candles I'd gotten at the army surplus store. George Thompson, our across-the-street neighbor, turned me on to the army surplus one day when I asked him if I could rake his lawn for a couple of bucks. He'd been sitting on his front porch in that rickety rocking chair, with his cane slung across his lap, watching me walk door to door, his Coke-bottle glasses following my every move.

When I asked him if he needed anything done, he told me to sit down, so I did. Since then, he'd gone completely blind, but we still talked. Every once in a while, he'd send me back to the house with sandwiches for Sam, too. He'd been a butcher for most of his life and knew a lot of things, the army surplus being one of them. You could get great deals on everything from pots to socks to candles to old rakes, and I went there before I went anywhere else when we needed stuff.

My half of the soup went quick, but it filled me up enough so I wasn't thinking about it all the time. What I did think about was what I'd like to do to Gary. We sat on the mattress Indian-style, and Sammy slurped the last of his soup while I shuffled a deck of cards. "Want to play?" I said.

"I want to go in."

"No."

"Why?"

"Because I said, Sammy. Now shut up and stop feeling sorry for yourself. It's not that bad. It's like a campout."

"Not even. Campers sleep in tents, not crappy sheds." He flung his thumb toward the house. "He doesn't live here. He should be the one to leave."

"You tell him that," I said, remembering how hard he'd squeezed my wrist.

"I'd just knock him over the head with something when he wasn't looking."

"Don't be dumb. Let's play." I dealt out the cards, and we played gin. I'd learned it from George before he'd gone completely blind, and I'd taught it to Sammy.

We played three games. I let Sammy win the last one because he usually got mad if he didn't. I put the cards back in the case and spread out our blankets. Music came from the house, and as I blew out the candles, I heard Mom laughing.

"Why'd you call me dumb?" Sammy curled up in the blankets.

"I didn't."

"Yeah, you did."

"I said, 'Don't *be* dumb.' That doesn't mean you *are* dumb."

"Elliot kicked me today."

"Why?"

"I don't know. He just did."

"What'd you do back?" I said. Sammy talked about Elliot bossing him around all the time, and even though Sammy was the biggest kid in class, it was like he had a sign around his neck that said BUG ME. They called him Patrick, from *SpongeBob SquarePants*.

Sammy didn't say anything for a moment. "Nothing."

"Don't let people push you around, Sam."

He raised his eyes to me. "I didn't let that stupid guard guy push me around, but then you got all mad."

"He wasn't pushing us around, Sam. He was just doing his job."

"So? We could skate there if we wanted."

"It's different, Sam. Now go to sleep."

He buried his head under the blanket. "That counselor guy says I shouldn't fight."

"You shouldn't."

"Then why are you mad I didn't get Elliot back?"

"Because there's a difference. And I'm not mad. You just have to take care of yourself, that's all."

"Mr. Franken says the school doesn't allow *any* fighting. Not even kicking. He says it's bad."

"You can fight *back*, Sam. It's called defending yourself. Elliot's a bully."

He shook his head under the blanket. "Nuh-uh. Mr. Franken says you should never fight. He says it just makes you just like the bad guy."

I settled in my blanket. "What was the name of the kid you got in the fight with before? The one that got you in with the counselor? Thomas?"

"Yep."

"You decked him, right?"

"Yep. His lip started bleeding all over, too."

"Does he bug you anymore?"

"No."

"Does he call you Patrick anymore?"

"No."

I nodded. "The only way Elliot will stop is if you make him.

32

Other people won't do things for you all the time, Sam. And Mr. Franken isn't going to be following you around all the time, is he?"

"I'll get in trouble if I fight."

I sighed. "Just don't go around picking fights, 'kay? And don't let Elliot push you around, either." We lay in the darkness for a few minutes, with Sam squirming all around beside me and driving me nuts. I heard him sniffle a couple of times. I rolled to face him and felt wetness on my arm from his cheek. "What's wrong, Sam?"

"I crossed you out on my picture today."

"I know."

"I was mad at you for saying stuff about Dad."

I put my arm over his shoulder. "That's okay, Sammy."

"Not really. It was mean. I shouldn't have done it." He sniffled.

"Maybe so, Sam, but don't worry about it. You're my bro, remember?" I squeezed him.

"Yeah. And bros are the best, right?"

I closed my eyes. "Yeah, Sam, bros are the best."

Chapter Five

With no electricity in the shed, I couldn't plug my alarm in, and with the prospects slim that some angel would come down and tap my shoulder at seven, I figured I'd be late to school. They locked the doors at 8:01, so I had to go to the office to check in, which meant another tardy and suffering through the highbrow sermonizing of the office steel fist, Mrs. Worthington. She liked me, though, and I knew when she told me to straighten up it was because she was like everybody's mother in a Nurse Ratched kind of way. This morning she simply notified me I would be meeting with Ms. Veer, the vice principal, later in the day.

Later turned out to be eleven, and after Ms. Veer showed me in, I took my usual spot in one of the padded chairs that wasn't quite as padded as those found in the principal's office. Ms. Veer looked around thirty-five years old and never wore pants. Always a skirt. She had a wide, flat butt, a tiny waist that went up to narrow shoulders, and a pointed, long face with a big-toothed smile. She didn't wear a ring on her finger, and the only picture on her desk was that of a horse with a blue ribbon attached to its neck. She stood beside it, a cowgirl hat on her head and a flannel shirt on, smiling her big-toothed smile as if she was the happiest person in the world.

I don't think she had kids, because she talked to me like I was either forty or four, and I'd bet my last nickel that if I'd told her I'd been late because I slept in a shed due to my mom's partying all night with a drug dealer, she would have followed procedural standards to a T and called Child Protective Services to file a report.

But her eyes were kind, and as the disciplinarian of the school, she caught you off guard because that look in her eyes didn't change, nor did the smile, even when she was giving you the shaft. The rules were the rules to Ms. Veer, and she didn't deviate from school policy. She was like a robot when it came to those things. I settled in, and she ruffled a few papers on her desk. "Ian, I'd like you to explain why you were tardy this morning. This is becoming a habit."

"I slept late," I said, wondering why she bothered with her usual chitchat before she swung the hammer.

She looked over her glasses at me. "I tried to call your mother, but the line was disconnected."

"She's arguing with the phone company about our bill, so they turned it off," I said, justifying the white lie because my mom argued with every bill collector in the city if they could get ahold of her. "My mom's stubborn."

"I see." She shuffled my file. "I'm allotting you three days' detention. We can't have students arriving late on a consistent basis. It is disruptive to the other kids."

"Okay."

She studied me, shrugging onto her desk with her gangly arms and smiling. This was a new angle, and she didn't do it very well. "Is everything going well at home, Ian?"

"Why?" *Why* was right, I thought. Ms. Veer *did not* talk personal stuff after she handed down punishment. It wasn't her style. Something was up.

Her eyes went to my file. "Well, I've talked to your counselor and he seems to think you are having a hard time here at Morrison. Many times that's indicative of a problem at home." She looked at my file again, and I realized she kept looking at it not because it contained anything she didn't already know but because she was nervous. "You did know that you, as a tenth grader, will be testing for the WAEE this year?"

I did. Washington state, along with the whole country, had to meet federal standards for learning, and besides the coveted rankings pitting schools against each other, they lost money and prestige if students didn't score well. The WAEE was the Washington Academic Evaluation Examination, and the tests were given in the fourth, seventh, and tenth grades. Kids who didn't pass them couldn't graduate with a regular diploma until they did. You could be an A student, but if you bombed the test, you'd get a big REJECT stamped on your forehead that would follow you around for the rest of your life. "Yes, I know about it."

She looked at my file again. "It's an important test, Ian. Your future hinges on it, and if there are stresses outside of the school that are distracting you, the consequences could be dire. We begin testing in one month, and Principal Spence is concerned."

Stresses outside the school. What a great way to put it. I wondered if she had a copy of *Warning Signs of Teenage Mental Problems for Dummies* in her drawer. "I'm fine."

Her eyes met mine in a goofy, knowing way, as if she understood what the deeper side of my life was about. "Do you know, Ian—I've been around the block a time or two. I see your test scores and I see the manner in which you conduct yourself at this school." She tapped the paper. "You've taken all general courses and done poorly on state and federal testing, though your aptitude scores tell a different story. You're highly intelligent. I might be wrong, but I get the impression you don't enjoy being here. I get the impression there might be issues in your life we here at Morrison might be able to help you with." She looked at me, hesitating for a moment before going on. "Either here or at an alternative school."

I shrugged. *Either here or at an alternative school* meant one thing at Morrison High unless you played sports. It meant, *We'll bug the hell out of you until you leave.* I had nothing to say to that, because I knew how things worked. Ms. Veer just didn't see it. Maybe she was too new to the school or maybe she was stupid, but it didn't matter. I knew how this school operated, and so did half the student body. You didn't fit the image, you were out.

"I'm here to help you, Ian. So is your counselor. Kerner Alternative is a great institution."

Kerner was for losers—pregnant girls and jerks and bangers and dysfunctional kids with nothing better to do than ruin their lives. "I don't need counseling or Kerner, Ms. Veer. Mr. Hacky is retiring next year anyway." What I needed, I thought, was three-fifty for dinner. Another three bucks would be nice for laundry, but I did have the sink.

"What does your counselor's retiring next year have to do with you?"

I laughed. "It means he talks more about the cabinets he's making in his garage than why a guy is late to school."

She gave me a look I didn't understand, and I got the uncomfortable feeling I'd been the topic of conversation elsewhere. "I think you're having trouble adapting to us, Ian. Have you thought about trying out for a sport at Kerner? I hear you are quite a runner, and you know, the athletic department at Kerner has an outstanding intramural program."

I thought of not doing push-ups anymore, then thought of Coach Schmidt getting creamed by a Mack truck, because I knew then that she'd talked to Ms. Veer about me. My counselor didn't have anything to do with it. "Then everything would be all right, Ms. Veer? I'd be all fine and dandy and on time to school and you wouldn't have to listen to Coach Schmidt bitch about how bad I'm screwing this school up?"

She tapped her finger. "I'm not understanding, Ian."

"I know you're not understanding."

She scribbled something on my file. "Would you explain, then?"

"Forget it."

A teeny bit of that kindness left her eyes. "You forget who you speak to, young man. It's my job to deal objectively with my students. As the main disciplinarian, I demand respect. You are accusing me of something, and I'm entitled to know what it is."

"Okay, fine. Coach Schmidt comes to your office yesterday and you two have a talk about me. She tells you she's tried and tried and tried to make me useful to this school, but I'm just too rebellious, right? It's just a lost cause. I mean, look at me, right? No polo shirt, no sandals, no nice and tidy haircut, right? Now you call me in and tell me that everything will be fine if I go to Kerner because they can 'help' me. Great. Sign me right up, Ms. Veer. I can't wait to have a perfect life."

Surprise lit in her eyes before she hid it. "Ian, I don't know where this is coming from, but—"

"Don't lie to me."

"Excuse me?"

"You can cut the bullshit out, Ms. Veer. I know how this school sees guys like me, so you can stop."

Her face darkened, and in an instant her smile was gone. "I can see how you might think that, but it's not the truth. Everybody has something to contribute, and we value everybody equally here."

"Is that straight from the handbook?"

"I won't stand insolence from you, and your sarcasm is out of line."

I riveted my eyes on hers. "Did Coach Schmidt talk to you?"

She hesitated. "No. Principal Spence did. Coach Schmidt spoke to him out of concern for you. So did Coach Florence."

"Same difference." I eyed her. "You don't get it, do you?"

"Get what, Mr. McDermott? That I take my job seriously and that you're not making any friends by mocking it?"

"No. That the only thing I want is to be left alone. I want to come to school, do my work, and go home. That's all. And you can sit there acting like you don't know what's going on here, but you and I both know the truth. This school wants me at Kerner for this school's benefit, not mine."

Her tone softened. "Coach Schmidt *has* mentioned you, Ian, and Principal Spence has brought you up to me several times. And though there may be some truth to what you say about this school, it is *my* job to make sure every student here is dealt with in a balanced and fair way." She paused, her eyes leaving mine and going to her hands on the desk. "I'm somewhat disappointed that your faith in this school, and me, is so low. You don't have to run for Morrison High if you choose not to, or apply yourself diligently to the WAEE, but I personally think you may be doing yourself a disservice. That being the case, I do want you to know that whatever your decision, my opinion of you will not change. I was concerned, Coach Schmidt was disturbed, and I felt it my duty to intercede." She studied me. "I think you should give some serious thought to Kerner."

I nodded, giving a small smile. She thought it was in my best interests? Baloney. Spence wanted me gone. "Okay."

She shrugged it off, turning her attention back to my file. "Well, we can't have you being late for class. One more time and I'll be forced to suspend you for three days. Hopefully detention will be a deterrent."

"Maybe I'll see Todd Haversham there, too?" I said. Todd played baseball *and* football for the Morrison Vikings, and I had first period with him. He'd been late too many times to count, and I hadn't seen him going to detention yet, much less heard about him being suspended. Guys like Todd Haversham somehow bypassed Ms. Veer and went straight to Principal Spence.

Her officiousness, and the tension around her mouth, came back in a flash. "This administration treats each circumstance as unique, and Mr. Haversham doesn't have anything to do with our conversation, Ian."

I left her office, and by then it was lunch. They had free lunch if you were eligible, but I wasn't. Mom hadn't filled out the paperwork, and that was a month ago, and I couldn't fill out the paperwork because it needed a parent's signature and proof of income. And while I could forge her signature almost perfectly, I had no idea about our income other than the checks Mom was always home for at the end of the month.

Usually I could scrape enough couch change for Sammy or work odd jobs around the neighborhood for cash, or Mom would slip me a ten, but lately there'd been no money. So I went to the library and stared at a book on genetic engineering for thirty-five minutes, thinking about Tony the day before and whether Veronica's lower half naked would be as nice as her upper half naked.

Veronica liked skate punks and, I've got to admit, I liked her. She's Daddy's million-dollar girl, has capped teeth and highlights in her hair, is a JV cheerleader, and does everything she possibly can to piss off her dad, who's a circuit court judge here in town. That would include letting me explore her Northern Hemisphere. Besides all that, though, she and I got along better than I would have ever thought. She's nice.

At the start, I took her interest in me to be more like the zoo visitor looking at the monkeys. Bennie said she was slumming, and I was wise to that from the start. Veronica had a reputation for picking just the wrong guys, and I was the next on her list.

Morrison High is unique in that a portion of its district dips down the hill, shoveling low-income students into the mix for the sake of cultural and economic diversity, which to me is nothing more than self-image enhancement for the rich. They look at the shit we don't have and feel good about what they do have.

After the library, Coach Schmidt ignored me during gym. Grateful for it, I slogged through forty-eight minutes of Ping-Pong and won every game. Woe be it to anybody challenging the Ping-Pong master, especially a five-foot-tall girl named Delores Braches who put in at a good one-seventy-five from the hips down and couldn't hit a beach ball with a paddle the size of her butt.

I hoped the guy with Mom was gone—but that Mom was still around—by the time Sammy and I got home. We needed money, and chances were I wouldn't be able to find any yards to rake before dark. I picked Sammy up, and he held a note from his teacher, explaining that Mom *needed* to contact the school. I had a feeling he might be held back if things didn't get better by the end of the year, but the only thing I could do was help him with his homework. God forbid I had enough time to do my own homework, but that was another story.

We walked for a while, not bothering with the boards, before Sammy spoke up. "I do try, you know," he said, and I knew he'd read the note. "It's just hard."

"I know. We just have to try harder."

"I'm dumb, Ian, and Elliot hit me again." Tears came to his eyes, and he wiped them on his sleeve. "I fell down on the playground, and he called me Patrick, so I called him a pecker, and he hit me."

"First of all, you're not dumb. And second of all, Elliot is an asshole."

He sniffled. "He told me I'm going to be in fourth grade forever, just like the niggers downtown."

"You're not going to be in fourth grade forever, Sam. Elliot's just a jerk. Kids like him have to say those things because it's the only way they can feel good about what they are."

"What's a nigger?"

I frowned. "Black people. It's like calling a black person the worst thing you can think of."

"I'm not a nigger, though. I'm white."

"I know. The guy across the street is a black guy."

"Mr. Thompson, the blind guy? He knows everything," Sammy said.

I nodded. "So don't go around saying that word. It hurts people." We walked, and after a block or two, Sam's sniffles went away. I kicked a pinecone. "I'll talk to your teacher about Elliot."

"No."

"What did your counselor say when you told him what happened?"

42

"I didn't tell."

"Why?"

"Elliot said he'd bust my arm if I told."

I stopped. "Next time Elliot does anything, you punch him. You're bigger than him, Sam, and the only way he's going to stop is if you beat him up. Don't stop punching, either. Keep doing it until he cries."

"I'll get kicked out. And besides, Mr. Franken says I'm higher than that."

"Just do it, Sam, okay? Guys like Mr. Franken don't know how it is sometimes."

"Okay." Then he brightened. "Hey, you think Mom will play Clue with us when we get home?"

"She might."

"Cool. I can prob'ly find those missing cards, too."

We got home, but the only sign of Mom was the casserole dish and plates caked with dried Tuna Helper. I threw them in the sink and the casserole dish cracked, leaving us with only a saucepan and pot to cook with. What a day. "Shit."

Sammy searched the house, then came into the kitchen, deflated. "Mom's gone."

"She might be back later. Get your homework."

He stood defiant. "I'm not doing it."

I could feel another episode coming, but I wasn't in the mood. "Yes, you are."

"No, I'm not. Mom's not here, and you can't make me. Nobody can make me do anything!"

I looked at our only casserole dish, now useless, and my chest tightened. "Yes, I *can* make you!" I turned around and exploded at him. "Mom is *always* gone, and when Mom's gone, *you do what I say!*" I picked up the cracked dish and threw it across the room.

43

It shattered against the refrigerator and sprayed glass all over the floor. "Do you want to live in a dump like this forever, Sammy?" I stared at him, with his big eyes and tears gathering at the corners, and it pissed me off even more. "*Do you?* Do you want to be a fucking beggar your whole life?"

He shook his head, scared out of his mind.

"Then do your homework!"

He stepped back, then his eyes went to the broken dish. Tears streamed down his face, and he looked at me. His eyes went back to the dish. "Don't be mad, Ian. I'm sorry. Really. We can fix that, you know. Just glue it or something." He ran over and fell to his knees, trying to fit the pieces together like a puzzle. He mumbled under his breath, picking up pieces and talking about how he could fix it.

I knelt beside him and my eyes stung. "Sammy, I'm trying here. I hate this as much as you do, but we can't change it. Not like this. We just have to work, see? Just work hard, and it'll be fine."

He didn't say anything, just picked up glass shards.

I took his hand away. "Don't, Sam; you'll cut yourself. It's fine. It is. We can get another one."

He gently laid the shards down and sat like a sad Indian, staring at me. "Why're you crying?"

I wiped my eyes. "I'm not. We'll just do your homework, okay? Then maybe play Clue, just you and me."

He smiled at that. "Maybe we can invite Mr. Thompson over to play, too."

I looked at him. "He's blind, Sam." I looked at him for a moment more before he smiled sheepishly, then we both busted up laughing.

Fifteen minutes into Sammy's homework, he told me he

didn't think we lived in a dump. I told him I didn't think so, either, and that I just got mad. We'd lived here for three years, and it was the best place yet. All the others had been apartments, and this was the first house. No yelling through the walls, no music thumping, no screaming kids.

Sammy finished his science. "What are we going to have for dinner?"

"We'll figure it out."

"Is that what you're mad about?"

"Sort of."

"You're mad at Mom, too, aren't you?"

Sometimes Sammy pegged it on the head. "Yes. I am."

"Because she's gone?"

"Because she's not here to play Clue with you."

"Don't be mad, Ian. We can play just like you said. Mom had to go. Prob'ly making money for bills and stuff."

I'd learned a long time ago that Mom will do what Mom does, and I can't do anything about it. Half the time I felt like she was a lost little kid, but it still made me mad. For Sammy. "Probably, Sam. And I'm not mad anymore."

"We could ask Mr. Thompson for dinner. We could even eat with him. I could hold his fork so he wouldn't poke himself on account of him not seeing and stuff."

I smiled. "We're fine, Sam. I'll get something." I stood. "You finish your math, and I'll be back." The clock read six-thirty, and the last streaks of red faded on the horizon. I walked toward the grocery store knowing I didn't have money to buy anything, but I couldn't think of anywhere else to go.

Chapter Six

Dinky's Food Mart is on the corner of Fiske and Sixth Avenue. The days were warming up, and the breeze blowing in my face held the last warmth before night's chill set in. I thought about Mom and that guy and wondered what she saw in him, but I knew. Drugs. Every guy she brought home seemed to have the same way about him, and I wondered if our dad had been that way, too. I didn't really remember his face, except for his eyes, and Mom never talked about him, but I've always pictured him as different. Better, maybe. But he'd left us, and I hated him sometimes. Not for leaving, because I understood why he'd do that, but for not taking us with him.

I thought about Sammy's picture on the refrigerator. Maybe that's why Dad had left, I thought. He'd wanted better, and with us, better wasn't an option. I did know that Mom started smoking dope around the time Sammy was born, and I figured she started after Dad left. Maybe to make herself feel better. I wondered sometimes, when I had time like this alone, if Mom had been on drugs with Sammy in her stomach. Maybe that's why he wasn't as quick, and that's why some things didn't click with him.

Mom and I never fought about things, and I guess I knew why. She tried the best she could and paid most of the bills she had to, but sometimes it all just fell apart. I'd seen her twice in two weeks and both times, especially the night before, she was there but not really there. Things just seemed to be slipping away, and I had a feeling we'd better get used to it.

I neared the grocery store and stood on the corner, watching people get out of cars and go inside. A few minutes later, they would come back out, bags in their hands, and drive off. Sammy needed food. I did, too. I walked around the parking lot searching absently for change, then watched a mother get out of her car with her daughter. Her purse dangled from her shoulder as she lugged the kid toward the store, and I wondered how much money she had in it. Probably enough for a dinner or two. Maybe more.

I turned around and walked deeper into the neighborhood, keeping my mind off the lady with the purse. Pools of light from the streetlamps reminded me of stage lights I'd seen at a school play once, and I walked around them. I didn't have anything for anybody to want, but getting jacked and beaten, even for nothing, happened enough around here to make habits.

I walked for ten minutes, then went back to the store. The lady with the kid and the purse was gone, and a new batch of cars were in the lot. I almost went inside, but I stopped, walking around the side of the building. Behind it, the alley was full of food racks and torn boxes and old shopping carts, their wheels broken and baskets bent.

I walked down the alley, my hands stuffed in my pockets,

47

stepping around the garbage and not knowing what I was doing. I couldn't go in the store. I had a nickel in my pocket. A wall light next to a metal employees' door illuminated smashed cigarette butts and Coke cans and plastic wrappers. A coffee can next to the door was full of more butts, and next to that, the green wall of a garbage Dumpster.

I peeked over the edge of the green thing and saw more boxes, plastic packing wrap, and garbage. The store usually had day-old baked goods on sale, and I wondered what they did with the expired stuff, so I hopped over the green wall and into the garbage. They probably gave it to a food bank or something, but I'd rather be a scrounger than a beggar. I glanced at the door, my feet crackling the packing plastic, hoping whoever smoked those cigarettes didn't come out.

Five minutes later, I'd found a half-crushed carton of dough-nuts, fished out a badly dented can of green beans, and stuck my hand in a broken jar of mayonnaise, cutting my thumb. As I got out, the back door opened and a girl, about twenty, appeared. She had an unlit cigarette between her lips and held a bottle of water. I hopped down, and she stared at me. I had mayo on my sleeve, blood dripping from my thumb, and the doughnuts and green beans balanced on the corner of the Dumpster.

She looked at me, her hand reaching for the door, but stopped when she connected my getting out of a garbage can with the food resting on the edge. She pursed her lips and put the smoke behind her ear, stuffing her lighter in her pocket. "Just a sec, 'kay?" she said, disappearing inside.

I didn't say anything, because I couldn't. I'd seen her at the checkout before, and I didn't know her name, but it didn't mat-ter. If there was a thousand-foot hole in front of me, I would have happily stepped into it, but something, maybe the way she smiled or how hungry Sammy was, kept me there. A minute later, she came back out with a can of Spam and a loaf of bread with a *Special* sticker on it. "We give it to the food bank anyway." She held it out to me.

I looked at her and wanted to run, but I couldn't go home with nothing for Sammy, so I took the stuff, putting the Spam in my pocket and tucking the bread under my arm with the crushed box of doughnuts. The green beans didn't fit anywhere, so I held them in my bleeding and mayonnaise-covered hand. She was pretty, and I wished she wasn't. "My brother is hungry."

She smiled. "Go feed him."

"Thank you."

When I got home, Ms. Veer, the vice principal, was sitting in our living room. Sammy sat in a cheapo white patio chair across from her. Mom's crack pipe lay on the coffee table. Ms. Veer stood when I came in, her eyes passing over my groceries without pause. "You're bleeding, Ian."

I looked at my thumb. "I cut it. It's fine." I walked to the kitchen and put the stuff in a cupboard.

She walked to the doorway. "I dropped by to talk to your mother." She smiled. "Your brother is a nice boy."

"She's not here."

"I know. Here." She took my arm and led me to the sink, ignoring the smeared mayo. "Does it hurt?" She turned the tap on, warming the water.

I took my hand away, sticking it under the water. It stung like a son of a bitch. "It's fine."

"Do you have any band . . . ," she started to say, then looked around the empty kitchen. "Here, let me." She squeezed some dish soap onto the cut and cleaned it out.

"I might have AIDS, you know."

She smiled. "I'm not worried. When is your mother going to be home?"

"Later tonight."

She nodded, grabbing the dish towel and patting my hand. "You won't need stitches."

I looked out the window, wishing she were anywhere but here.

"Hold the towel over it with pressure and it will be fine."

"Why are you here?"

She rested her hand on the counter. "I wanted to meet your mother to talk about our conversation."

"Well, she's not here."

"I realize that. Your brother told me she's gone quite often." She gave me a soft, questioning look. "Maybe too often?"

"Not really. She works sometimes and gets home late. After he's asleep."

She nodded to the cupboard. "You brought home dinner?"

"I fell on the way home. That's why the stuff got smashed." I held up my finger. "How I cut my finger, too. Sorry she's not home. I'll tell her you dropped by."

"That would be good. I'd like to talk to her."

I walked her to the door. "Bye."

She said goodbye to Sammy, then looked at me with something close to regret in her eyes. "I've rescinded your detention, Ian."

"Why?"

"You pick your brother up every day after school?"

I nodded.

She nodded, too. "Good night, Ian."

"Good night."

Chapter Seven

At ten-fifteen the next morning, Mr. Spence called me into his office. In his midforties and with an executive's haircut and immaculate suit, he ushered me into his throne room. He had a round face, a sharp nose, and graying temples and reminded me of a church guy. "Have a seat."

The office was bigger than Ms. Veer's, and the chairs softer. Mr. Spence had a picture of his family—three older boys all with the same look about them and one holding a football—sitting on his desk next to a miniature bust of Thomas Jefferson. As I took a seat, I wondered if Mr. Jefferson had played ball, too. He was probably the star quarterback of the Colonial Patriots or something.

I looked closer at the picture. His wife was pretty but had a stern set to her lips, and I wondered if she was nice. Next to that, a stapler, a pen holder, and a coffee mug with *Vikings* slashed across it sat half empty. I noticed he took cream with his coffee. Behind him, several certificates hung on the wall.

He fiddled with a red and silver pen, adjusted a pair of reading glasses on his nose, and began. "Ms. Veer spoke with me this morning, and she is concerned about your welfare here at Morrison." He looked at me. "She visited your home last night?"

"My welfare here?"

"Yes, Mr. McDermott. Your welfare here. She's concerned." My test scores sat on top of my file, and he set them aside, picking up my discipline file. "You've been in my office three times since you were a freshman and had numerous infractions, including detention and one suspension. All have involved conflict with the teaching staff, not the student body. This tells me you have a problem with authority, Mr. McDermott, and though I appreciate Ms. Veer's concern, I see the school doing its duty as dictated by the district, and a student who is indifferent to receiving a superb education. You do know that Morrison High has been rated in the top one hundred high schools nationwide?"

I shrugged. Ms. Veer.

He smirked, irritated. "That's the attitude I'm talking about, Mr. McDermott, and as it continues, I don't see your stay here as being beneficial." He paused. "To you or the school. And with the road you've chosen, I think certain alternatives might be best."

"I was late."

"I'm not talking about being tardy, Mr. McDermott. I'm talking about *our* outlook on education as opposed to *yours*. Other philosophies may be better suited to one such as yourself. Perhaps Rolling Hills Alternative or Kerner might be best."

"Best for me or best for you?"

He grimaced, folding his hands like a preacher readying himself to sermonize. "You do not respond to authority, you have no interest in school activities, you've defied nearly every teacher you've had over mundane, childish issues, and I'm not seeing a team player here. I'm seeing a pattern of behavior leading to a situation I won't have at my school. In fact, Coach Schmidt came to see me yesterday, just as Coach Florence has in the past." A distasteful look came to his face when he spoke Schmidt's name. It was common knowledge that he didn't enjoy having the first female head football coach in high school history. "She seems to think you are a distraction to the students who want to learn, and I can't have that. She can't, either."

Principal Spence leveled a stare at me. He tapped his pen on the desk, waiting for me to say something. Nothing came. "Coach Schmidt takes her job seriously, Mr. McDermott, and I cannot allow you to constantly defy and mock her resolve in supplying the students here with the best direction possible. You were outwardly aggressive toward her the other day, and Coach Florence has made numerous comments to me about your volatility. And I don't need to remind you that I will use the law to its fullest degree if another assault occurs."

"I didn't assault Coach Schmidt. I took her hand from me. And Coach Florence hassles me every time he gets the chance. He hates my guts."

Mr. Spence looked me over. "We're not in the business of being friends. We're educators."

"Tell him that, then."

He raised his eyebrows, thrusting his chin out and nodding. "I see. I can understand his frustration with you."

"What's that supposed to mean? That you understand he's a prick?"

He sat back in his chair, and I think if he'd had a gavel he would have pounded it on the desk. "It means you are not right for this school, Mr. McDermott, and I think you and your mother should investigate an alternative before you cause more harm

53

here. The district tries very hard to place students such as yourself in an appropriate manner. There are opportunities for you elsewhere, young man."

I knew Spence was lying. Coach Schmidt would never duckwalk into his office and tell him she was afraid of me. I might not like her much, but I knew her enough to know. She'd mentioned it to him, and now he was using it for his own benefit. "I didn't assault anybody. I was late to school."

Mr. Spence looked at me with indifference. "I don't believe your outlook is conducive to a safe, stable environment needed for teaching, and as you know, things have changed since all of these school shootings." He shook his head, then lowered his eyes to me. "I am the deciding factor in whether or not you step foot on this property. As you must know, this is a tremendous responsibility, which I value greatly." He paused. "I have concluded *and* documented, from speaking with Coach Florence, Coach Schmidt, and Vice Principal Veer, that you are a security risk, Mr. McDermott, and it's my job to keep this school safe."

I looked at him, confused. "What, you think I'm going to shoot the place up or something?" I furrowed my brow, thinking of those two kids in Colorado. I might wear black and get around on a skateboard, but I wasn't a mass killer.

"Are you making a threat?"

"No, I just don't know what you're talking about."

Mr. Spence's eyes darkened. "I'll make it simple, then. I don't want you at my school, Mr. McDermott. You don't fit, and I don't see a need for you to continue here."

I raised my voice. "Because I don't wear a jacket and play sports and have rich parents?" I don't know how many times I'd seen teachers single out my friends and hassle them, and now this asshole was doing it to me. "Tell me why."

"Because I'm cleaning up this school."

"Then suspend me. Call the police. Prove it."

He sat back, tossing his pen on the desk. "As I said, you openly defied Coach Schmidt yesterday, and if I weren't looking out for your well-being, what you did could be classified as an assault on a teacher. I need say no more."

"Go ahead, then. Do it. Press charges. I don't give a shit what you do."

He shook his head. "I'm giving you a chance here, young man. A chance to start new. Somewhere else." He looked at me like he really thought he was doing me a favor. "Someplace where you could blend in. Give some thought to what I told you. There are many vocational trade classes available at Kerner that would be applicable for a person with your aptitude, and I'm afraid your continuance at this school will not benefit you." He stopped, regarding me for a moment. "I can guarantee it, actually."

"Are we done?"

"I will have my assistant draw up the papers for a transfer. Dismissed."

I saw Ms. Veer in the hall outside Mr. Spence's office, and she was all smiles. "Did you talk to Principal Spence?"

"Yes."

She looked at me. "What's the matter?"

"Don't come to my house anymore."

She looked confused. "What did Mr. Spence say?"

"Forget it. Just leave us alone." I left her speechless and didn't care. They always had something to say, and I didn't give a goddamn about any of it, anyway.

My stomach did somersaults during lunch hour. I didn't want

to see Coach Schmidt or Coach Florence next period, but I would. I should have skipped. I don't know why I didn't. I should have.

When I came in the gym, Coach Schmidt was opening the locker room doors and some guys from class were waiting to suit up. I tried to walk by without her noticing me, but she did. I should have taken Mr. Spence's advice and walked out. Schmidt put the keys in her pocket and folded her arms. "Suit up, Ian."

I looked at her standing there and knew right then, by the look in her eyes, that she didn't know what had happened. There had been no plan other than Spence's plan. I knew she'd gone to him, probably irritated or pissed, and talked with him about me. I also knew that Ms. Veer had gone to Spence after visiting my house last night, and when she'd talked to him, he'd seen an opportunity. To "clean up" the school.

I knew Principal Spence didn't like Coach Schmidt one bit. Hardly anybody did. She was a woman, she coached football, and more than that, everybody saw her as a dyke, which, for all I knew, she was. Coach Florence would barely nod at her when they passed, and you could almost see the contempt and embarrassment on his face when she, as the Director of Athletics at Morrison, gave him an order in front of students. Suddenly I saw the road she'd traveled, and I wondered if in some ways it was the road Bennie was starting on.

I remembered what Spence told me. *I'm cleaning up this school.* I remembered the office staff looking at me when I came out, like they knew what was happening, and I remember wanting to run. I could also picture Coach Florence smiling with those ultra-white teeth as I left campus for the last time.

As I stood there looking at Coach Schmidt and wondering why she'd ever want to be a football coach and become the pariah of nearly every male coach in the world, Coach Florence walked in from the gym spinning a key on his finger. We'd be starting basketball today, and Florence headed up my class for that. He looked my way as he walked, his lanky legs swallowing ground with every step, and stopped. "Hey, McDermott." He threw the key toward me. "Get the balls from the cage and get suited up."

I caught the key and looked at him. Then I looked to Coach Schmidt. Freshmen were the gofers for coaches during class, and for the last fifty-seven years, freshmen had gotten the balls from the ball cage for the upperclassmen to warm up with. I was a sophomore. Coach Schmidt gave me a bullshit look like she couldn't do anything. She could. She could tell him to lay off, and I couldn't help but think about our conversation the day before. Respect.

I told him no.

He frowned, pointing a finger at me. "You get the balls, and you get them now, do you understand me?"

I stared at him, and Principal Spence loomed in my head: *for a person with your aptitude.* I knew exactly what he was saying. I wasn't the player, I was the loser getting the balls from the cage. I was the pizza delivery guy, the garbage man, and the gardener. I was below, and he was above. I glanced over and saw Bennie, who slowly shook his head in warning. I looked back to Coach Florence. "Freshmen get the balls from the cage."

He smiled. "No, you do."

I threw the key at his feet. Coach Schmidt shuffled nervously, telling students to go get dressed. None did. Florence stepped closer and pointed a finger again, this time inches from my nose. "You get the balls or you get your ass out of *my* gym, you got it? Pick up the keys!"

57

Over thirty guys and girls from the class formed a packed ring around us as Coach Florence backed up a half step and pointed to the key on the floor. *"Pick it up!"*

"Fuck you."

Coach Florence's eyes widened, then narrowed as he clenched his jaw. "What?"

"I said, *'Fuck you.'* Pick it up yourself." The class went dead silent. I didn't care. I didn't care about anything but that I'd had enough. *I'm cleaning up this school.* Fine. He'd won. I was done. I turned to walk out, and Florence grabbed my shoulder, swinging me around.

I hit him.

I threw a roundhouse and hit him square on the jaw. He fell like a lead weight, and my knuckles throbbed enough to know I'd done some damage. Major damage. Coach Schmidt, who up until then had stood mute, took a step forward. I faced her. "You could have stopped him!" I yelled. "You could have, you bitch! I was leaving!" I looked at Florence. He was out. Completely out. Bennie gaped.

Coach Schmidt had a look on her face that I couldn't read. Sad or mad, she didn't let on, but I did see a flicker of something I didn't like. Fear. "Go, Ian. Get out," she whispered, her voice low.

I did. I ran. I ran until I realized I didn't have anywhere to run to, then stopped. I was near Sammy's school. Then I looked behind me. Bennie was a block away, huffing and puffing and windmilling his skinny legs after me. I knew what would happen now. I would be arrested. Child Protective Services would take Sammy to foster care, and when I got out of juvie, we wouldn't be together. Ms. Veer had seen the crack pipe. My mother was an addict. My life was over.

Bennie caught up with me, breathing like an asthmatic, then

fumbled in his pocket for a cigarette. He lit up, and we walked. "Remind me never to piss you off, man," he said.

"Knock it off, Ben. My life just flushed down the toilet."

He laughed. "You laid him out. Dude, I *never* thought I'd see that guy on the floor. Sort of liked the look of it."

I turned to him. We were almost at Sammy's school. "You don't get it, Bennie, do you? I'm gone. Mom's gone. Ms. Veer came to the house last night and saw a crack pipe on the table. She *knows*, man."

He stared at the ground, the gelled railroad spikes he had for hair glistening black in the sun. "Sammy."

"Yeah, Sammy." I kicked a rock and watched it bounce off the chain-link fence ringing the playground.

"You guys could stay at my place. Dad works like a billion hours, and he'd never even know you were there. Besides, he'd probably be cool with it, anyway. You'd have to get used to two dudes knocking boots through the walls, though. Sorta freaky, really."

I shook my head. "They'd find me, Ben. They'd find Sammy." I left him standing at the curb and went into the office, explaining that our mother was in the hospital and that I needed to take Sammy there. She'd been in a car wreck, I said, and the lady oooohed and oh-no'd before calling Sammy from class.

We met Bennie at the curb and started walking. Bennie lit another smoke. "Hey, shrimp."

"I don't live in the ocean," Sammy said, then turned to me. "Mom didn't get into an accident, did she?"

"No."

"I was sort of wondering. She doesn't have a license. Or a car anymore."

"Nope."

"Why did you get me?"

"We've got to go."

Bennie piped up. "Ian kicked Coach Florence's ass. Flattened him like a pancake."

Sammy's eyes widened. "Really?"

I shook my head. "Ben . . ."

Bennie bobbed his head, then shrugged. "Well, you did."

"Where are we going, Ian?"

"I don't know."

"You really decked him?" Sammy's eyes widened.

I nodded.

"The cops are gonna come, then. Mr. Franken says when you hit an adult, you go to jail," Sammy said, looking around.

"Yeah. And when they take me, they'll take you, Sam."

"I didn't do anything wrong. They can't."

"They can."

"Mom'll stop them."

I stopped walking, facing my brother. "Sammy, Mom's not around. And even if she was, they'd take you."

"Why?"

I started walking again. I wasn't about to explain what Ms. Veer saw, and Mom probably not even showing up for hearings and everything else to get him back. "We just have to go."

Sammy's voice turned squeaky, and tears came to his eyes. "I want Mom."

I turned around, wishing everything could be as simple as he thought. Mom couldn't fix anything. Mom never fixed anything, and the only person who did fix things was me, and I'd screwed it all up. I grit my teeth, trying to keep my temper, but it didn't work. "I messed up, okay? I'm sorry. I shouldn't have hit him, but

I did and now we have to go. Mom can't change any of that." I threw my board down. "Mom can't change anything, Sammy!"

Sammy's crying didn't stop like it usually did when I got mad. His eyes darkened and he balled up his fists. "You shut up! And don't talk about Mom that way! You're the one who decked that guy, and she didn't do anything. You're the stupidhead, Ian! You're the one who always messes things up!"

"Fine! Stay! See how you like sitting in some shelter until they find you a foster home! You know what happens in shelters, Sam? Bad stuff. Stuff you don't even want to think about and stuff that makes Elliot look like the nicest kid in the world!" I walked on alone, Sammy standing on the sidewalk with tears running down his cheeks and Bennie standing next to him. I didn't look back, my own eyes burning. A minute later, I heard footsteps behind me.

It was Bennie. Sammy still stood where I'd left him. "Dude, you can't leave him there."

"What should I do, then, Ben? Pick him up and carry him? I'm not his dad, man. I'm not."

"You guys *really* could stay with us. It'd work. I could hide you."

I looked at Sammy, then back to Ben. "I'm not stupid, Ben. What I did to Florence is a felony, man, and I *know* Ms. Veer saw the pipe. You really think my mom would be able to show for my hearing and Sammy's hearing and do everything to get him back? They make you go through rehab and counseling and a bunch of other shit, Ben. She can't even be home, let alone show up for things. She's barely functional."

He shrugged. "I don't know, Ian, but you've got to do something."

61

"I am."

"Running?"

I stared at him. "What else is there, Ben? You remember Chris Perez? What about Chelsea Laughlin?" I kicked the curb. "Chris got screwed by his foster father for two years before anything happened, man, and there isn't a chance in hell I'll put Sammy into that. Chelsea's foster mom beat the crap out of her every time the wind blew. And besides, Sammy can't take care of himself like other kids. He needs me."

Ben lit a cigarette. "What are you going to do, then?"

"Skate out, man. We're going."

He shrugged, looking back at Sam. "Your choice, then. Get your brother, though. He's scared."

I looked at Sammy standing there with his arms crossed, then walked to him. He didn't budge. "I'm sorry, Sam."

"I want Mom."

I shook my head, then knelt in front of him. "I don't think Mom can help, Sam. I don't even know where she is. But if they catch us, we won't be together anymore, and I don't want that. Do you?"

He shook his head.

"Then come with me?"

His chin quivered. "Where are we going?"

"I don't know yet. We have to go home and get some stuff, though."

"Maybe Mom'll be there." He nodded, and we walked back to Ben. We started toward the house, and I made a mental check-list of what we might need. But the biggest empty spot on the list was money. I had a nickel in my pocket, and we had half a loaf of bread and one doughnut left from the night before.

We rounded the corner of our block, and a patrol car idled in front of the house. That meant Mom wasn't home, and a part of me was glad because of it. She wouldn't have been able to do a thing, anyway. "Crap," I said. "They're waiting."

Bennie stood staring at the car, then turned to me, digging in his pocket. He pulled out three bucks. "That's all I got, man. Got busted for smoking pot again, and Dad cut the purse strings."

I nodded and stuffed the dough in my pocket.

Ben smiled. "That cop doesn't know what you look like."

"So?" I said.

"So what if he thinks I'm you?"

"You'd get arrested, Ben, and besides, I'm way taller than you."

He smirked. "So what? Ever know a cop that didn't chase a kid running away from him? He'll take the bait, chase, catch me, find out I'm not you, and let me go. Gets them off your back for a while, and I have some fun."

"You sure?"

He shrugged, smiling wickedly. "When you've got a guilt-laden homosexual for a father, you can get away with all sorts of shit. He can just double his 'how to deal with a mixed-up child' counseling sessions for a few weeks. No problem."

"Up to you, Ben."

He slapped my shoulder, stretching his legs melodramatically. "It ain't illegal to run, is it?" He smiled. "You need anything at all, you come to my place, okay?"

"Thanks, Ben," I said, watching him walk toward the cop. Half a block away, the cop noticed Ben and stared suspiciously. Then Ben bolted, running for the vacant lot around the corner. The cop turned his lights on and chased.

When the cop turned the corner, we went to the house. I told Sammy to empty his backpack and put his jacket and a change of clothes in it. I did the same with an old pack from the closet, then went to the kitchen. I grabbed the lighter, a can opener, and the bread and doughnuts and scanned the drawers, taking the small saucepan, a spoon and fork, and the biggest knife we had. I stuffed them in my pack, which barely held it all, and went to the shed, sticking the candles and deck of cards in an outside pocket.

Sammy had his things together and had room in his pack, so I stuffed a blanket inside his. "Take your skullcap. It might rain." I grabbed mine, which wouldn't even fit unless I washed the spikes from my hair, and put it in his pack. I looked around the house, trying to think of anything else we might need, but we didn't have space anyway. Hell, I thought, I didn't even know where we were going. Away. Just away. Then I remembered the map.

We'd almost taken a trip two years ago to Seattle, when Mom had a car, and she'd bought a map of Washington. She'd called the three-day trip a grand adventure, promising to show us the neighborhood she'd grown up in, called the U District, and also take us to the wharf to eat seafood. The day before the trip, she was picked up for driving under the influence. They impounded the car, and we stayed home. Three weeks later, she sold it for two hundred bucks' worth of drugs.

I went to the kitchen and found the map in the utility drawer, where I kept my tools: a pair of pliers, a screwdriver or two, a small pipe wrench, and tape. I folded the map and stuck it in my back pocket, then found Sammy in Mom's room. He was sitting on the bed. "We've got to go, Sam."

"I don't want to. I just think we should wait for Mom. Really. I do."

"We'll call her."

"You said the phone doesn't work."

"We have to go." The house was quiet. Sammy started crying

again. I sat next to him and put my arm around his shoulder. "We'll come back. We will. When things get better."

"When?"

"I don't know. But we will. I promise." I hugged him. "We have to be strong, Sammy. Just like Mom used to say. Remember?"

"No."

He didn't remember because she hadn't ever said that. "Well, she did. She used to say you always had to be strong when things got bad, and she always said you were strong."

Sammy crossed his arms. "We have to say goodbye."

"Sammy . . ."

"I'm not going unless we say goodbye. I'm staying right here until Mom comes home." He sat defiant, his jaw set.

I tapped my toe, thinking and looking out the window. The cops would come back. "Okay, Sam. We'll find her." I picked up his pack. "We'll find her, say goodbye, then we go. Deal?"

"Are you lyin'?"

"Do I lie?"

"Sometimes."

"Do I lie to you?"

"No."

"Okay, then, come on." I helped him with his pack and slung mine over my shoulder. We grabbed our boards and set off, not knowing where we were going, but going nonetheless.

Chapter Eight

Vice Principal Veer rounded the corner in her car just as Sammy and I shut the front door. "Crap," I said. Sammy waved. "Ignore her, Sammy."

"But she was nice, Ian. . . . Maybe she could—"

"Please. Just do it. Just walk." I led him from the porch, and she pulled her car next to the curb and opened her door.

"Ian?" She held her keys and left her car door open as she hurried after us. "Ian, please, stop."

I stopped.

"Where are you going?"

"What do you want?" I could tell she was upset.

"I know what happened, Ian. Coach Florence is on the way to the hospital."

"Good."

She studied me for a moment, doubt crossing her face. She looked to her car.

"You want to go, so go," I said. "You don't owe me anything."

"That's not it, Ian. Really. I want to fix this. It *can* be fixed, but we've got to do this the right way. Please." When she said "please," it was with a pleading smile. I couldn't stand the sight of it.

"What right way? Your right way?" I shook my head. Ms. Veer knew only one way to do things. The rule-book way.

Her always-there smile faded. "*The* right way, Ian."

"No."

Her eyes met Sammy's, then switched to me. "What are you going to do? Run away? Is that the answer?"

I studied her face. "People like you have no idea what you do to people like me, Ms. Veer. You're dealing with your job. That's all. Nothing more. You'll go home, go to bed, get up, and go back to work. Big deal. Another problem *dealt* with. Another file passed on to the next person because that's what somebody decided should happen." I shook my head. "This is my life. *Our* lives, and I just fucked it up. And for you to stand there and act like we'd wake up tomorrow morning in the same house in the same beds and *deal* with this problem like you would is ridiculous. *You're* ridiculous."

She brought her shoulders back a bit, defensive. "I don't expect that, Ian, but every action has consequences, some harsher than others. I'm here because I may have pushed you too hard. Those are my consequences, and I really—"

"Don't tell me about consequences."

"I can help you. We can straighten this mess out and get back on track."

"What track?" I exploded. "What, Ms. Veer? The track where I end up in juvie and Sammy ends up in some home and we don't see each other anymore? That track? Sammy needs me."

"It doesn't have to be that way."

"Sure. Just like you coming to see my mom was supposed to be another way? Just like that fucker Spence telling me to get out of Morrison was supposed to be another way?" I glared at her. "You got played, Ms. Veer, and Florence and Spence and Morrison High got what they wanted. Big deal. Morrison doesn't want trash, and I'm not the first to go. I don't need this. Sammy doesn't, either." I spit. "And we were fine before you decided to stick your nose in things, so if you want to feel sorry for someone, feel sorry for yourself, because if you think you're helping things, you're an idiot."

"I *do* want to help, and there are ways we can help effectively. You're a bright young man, Ian, and running away doesn't solve anything."

I looked around at this neighborhood that made me feel the way I did. "Bright doesn't matter here, Ms. Veer, and you don't want to help me. You want to help yourself. So stop acting like you can make a difference, because you can't."

"That's not true." She drew herself up.

I stared at her. "Tell me you weren't going to call CPS after you saw the pipe."

She sighed.

"You called them, didn't you?" I smiled.

She clenched her jaw. "That's my job, Ian. I felt it necessary to intervene. You can't be around this. It isn't healthy."

"Well, I *am* around this! And you don't know shit about our lives, so why don't you get back in your nice little car and drive back to your nice little school and forget it! We don't need you or anybody else who thinks they know what's best screwing things up! Florence has had it out for me since the first day he saw me, and I'm glad I hurt him. He's a prick, and Spence is right—I *am* a security risk." I took a step toward her, and her hand moved toward the cell phone at her waist. "Go ahead!" I yelled. "Call! Call the cops, Ms. Veer! That's what helping is, right?"

She was scared. I saw it in her eyes. "I'm not calling the police, Ian. I know you won't hurt me, and I know that's not true."

"Then leave us alone."

"Will you tell me where you're going?"

I didn't answer. Sammy shuffled behind me.

She unclipped the phone. "Take this." She held it out.

I didn't take it.

"I'm not going to do anything, Ian. I want you to trust me. Just take it. I won't call you or anything. You call me, okay?"

"Why?"

The look in her eyes wasn't anything like the one she had in the picture on her desk—the one with the horse and ribbon and goofy, bucktoothed grin. "Because something terribly wrong happened here, and it's not all your fault. I'm not giving up on this. Or you." She put the phone in my hand. "Call me, Ian. Please. Don't throw your life away." She looked at Sammy, then turned to her car.

I stood and watched her drive away. "Let's go, Sam."

"Mom?" he said.

"Yeah. Mom."

"Where is she?" Sammy asked.

"I don't know. Maybe Bernie's."

"Bernie's?"

"It's a bar. We'll try there first." I'd heard Mom talk about Bernie's before.

"Ms. Veer seems like she really wants to help us, Ian. Maybe you should call." Sammy flipped his board up and carried it. I did the same.

"No."

"Why?"

"Because people like her don't know."

"Know what, Ian?"

I thought about Morrison High's kind of help. *I'm cleaning up this school.* "Their way of helping is to get us out of the way, and that's not going to happen."

"Really?" He furrowed his brow. "I don't think she'd do that."

I shrugged. "She did do that, Sam. People can talk nice and be mean at the same time."

"You said mean things to her. And you called her an idiot."

"I was mad."

"Why?"

"Let's stop talking, okay? We're almost there."

Three men sitting on bar stools stared at me when I walked through the door of Bernie's, and I knew by their jackets that the Harleys parked outside, the ones Sammy sat next to right now, were theirs. One smoked a cigar, and the smoke made a white haze against the dark of the place.

The bartender eyed me when I came to the counter. "Lost?"

"I'm looking for Naomi McDermott."

He smiled. "Didn't know she took youngsters on." He glanced at the men in front of their beers. "Times must be tough, huh, Frank?"

Frank laughed.

"She's my mother."

His smile disappeared, and he scratched his ear. "Didn't mean nothing by that, kid. Just foolin'. Besides, she ain't here."

My stomach trembled. "Do you know where she is?"

"Last I saw, she was with Malachi Jordan." He wiped the bar. "Lives over on Sixth and Horton. Green house."

70

"Thanks."

"I see her, I'll tell her you were in."

Sammy was sitting on the curb when I came out, and we hopped on our boards, heading for Malachi Jordan's green house on Sixth. I thought about Ms. Veer and what Sammy had said. I'd put the phone in my pack but was tempted to throw it away. She couldn't help, and I wasn't an idiot. Being nice didn't make things better.

Green wasn't exactly the color of the house. Blotchy ivy covered half the siding, and where it didn't, the siding was falling off, the bare walls underneath looking like pale scabs. The ivy came from an old lattice covering the porch, and down the steps were a few banged-up garbage cans spilling over with trash. I left Sammy on the sidewalk and jumped over garbage to get to the porch, where the doorbell had a weathered square of paper taped over it, reading DON'T BOTHER.

After the fifth knock, a shirtless man with a scraggly beard and pockmarks on his neck opened the door, squinting in the sunlight. Oily streaks of hair ran down to his shoulders. "What?"

"Are you Malachi?"

"Who're you?" he said, rubbing his eyes, then scratching his scrawny, hair-covered chest. His eyes, set deep, focused on me, blinking away sleep.

"Ian McDermott."

"I ain't buying anything."

"I'm looking for Naomi McDermott. Is she here?"

"Ain't none of your business who's here and who's not."

"She's my mom." I pointed to Sammy on the curb. "We need to see her."

"Ain't my problem. Get off my porch."

"Is she here?"

He poked his head through the rip in the screen door. "You hear me? Get out. She ain't your business."

"I need to talk to her."

He moved to shut the door, and I put my hand through the ripped screen, holding it open. He pushed harder, cussing that he'd beat me up if I didn't get off his property. I opened the screen with my other hand and jammed my foot against the door, shoving it open. Malachi lost his balance, tripping on an old bowling bag and sprawling on his back.

He scrambled up, knocking a coat tree over and making a racket. Then I saw Mom walking up the hall, her hair all mussed and her makeup smeared. I called to her, but Malachi steadied himself on the door and shoved. I shoved back.

Malachi grabbed my hair, yanking me forward, while Mom yelled for him to let go. Bent over with his fist buried in my hair, I threw a hard uppercut and felt it connect, sinking deep in his gut. I smelled liquor on his breath as he let go, doubling on his knees in front of me.

Mom screamed as I followed him down, rabbit-punching the top of his skull and following through with a quick blow to his ear before I knocked him back with my knee. He lay there, his chest heaving as he tried to catch his breath, his eyes wide and riveted on my face. I raised my fist and he held his breath, motionless as I knelt over him.

Mom had her hand over her mouth, looking at me as if I was the most horrible thing she'd ever seen. I stood up, facing her. "We can't go home. Sammy's outside. He needs you." I turned on my heel and left her there, walking back to Sammy. His eyes were glued on Mom, and as I reached him, he yelled for her. Then I heard Malachi cuss, and the door slammed shut. "Be quiet, Sam. She'll come out."

"She said she'd come out? She did?"

I sat down on the sidewalk, rubbing my head in my hands. "Yeah. She's got to get ready."

Sammy sat down next to me Indian-style, picking at dandelions growing through the cracks in the sidewalk. "You okay?"

I rubbed my hand. "Yeah."

"You beat the crap out of him."

"He didn't want us to see Mom."

He perked up. "She saw me. I waved to her while you were punching that guy."

I laughed. "Good, Sam. No worries."

"I wish I could beat up Elliot like that. Or send him to Mars."

I looked at him. "Mars is better."

Sam and I sat on the sidewalk until I counted seventeen dandelion heads in his pile. At least a half hour. Mom was hopeless, and I was an idiot for thinking she would come out. She had one thing, and that one thing had her. Drugs. "We've got to go, Sam."

He looked at his pile. "You said I could say goodbye." He shook his head. "I didn't."

"She's not coming out."

"Yes, she will. You said she has to get ready. She always takes a million hours anyway."

"No." I watched an old lady walk down the street, a grocery bag set in the basket of her walker.

"She knows we're here. She saw me. She'll be out in a minute. I know she will."

"Mom's sick, Sam. She can't." I picked up his pile of dandelion heads and threw them on the yard. "Come on."

"She'll come out!" Tears welled in his eyes. He stared at the door. "She will, Ian. You said so."

"She's too sick."

He cried harder. "She's not sick, Ian! I saw her! She looked right at me, and you said she's coming out. Maybe she fell asleep or something and we should wait."

Dust on his cheeks made streaks from the tears, and I almost started crying, too. "We have to go, Sammy. I'm sorry."

"Maybe he won't let her out, Ian. Maybe she's in trouble. You should go in again and beat him up more. Kill him or something. Then she'll come out."

I picked up his pack. "No."

"No!" he shrieked. "She'll come out! She will! I know she will!"

I grabbed his sleeve, and he yanked away, kicking me in the shin and running for the door. I yelled after him, then followed, tackling him at the stairs and pinning him. He kicked and tried to bite me. I stared into his face from an inch away, and I could see a million miles into his eyes. *"Sam! She doesn't want us!"* I pulled him up and he went slack, so I yanked him up and carried him to our packs. He sniffled, staring at the door as I put his pack on, all the fight gone from him.

Chapter Nine

"**Y**ou're a bastard."

Sammy hadn't said a word since we left Mom, and now, at the edge of town, he'd just called me a bastard. Tired of skating, we walked.

"Maybe I am," I said.

"Well, you are."

"Why a bastard?"

He kicked a rock. "Because that's the worst name I know besides *nigger*, but that's the worstest, and you'd prob'ly beat me up like you beat everybody else up if I said it."

"I'd never beat you up, Sam. No matter what."

"I'm scared."

"Me too."

Elms, willows, and maple trees grew over the cracked sidewalks, spring leaves shading us from the sun as we walked, and soon we came to a dead end. Beyond the rusted wire fence, pasture and scrub pine dominated, with a railroad track slicing off to the southwest. Three or four old farmhouses, set far apart, checkered the landscape. From there, pine-covered hills rolled up the valley, with the four-lane highway snaking straight south.

We stood at the fence, a sick knot in my stomach as I thought about what lay ahead.

"What're we doing?" Sammy said.

I looked south, over the fields. "We're going to find Dad."

"Dad? You mean *our* dad?"

"Yeah."

"You don't even know where he is. We don't even know him. I never even seen his picture."

"I know where he lives. He wrote Mom a letter once."

"Really?"

"Yeah. I saw it in the mailbox and memorized the address. It's easy. 1313 North Thirteenth Street."

"Wow. What's his name?"

"Samuel."

"Hey . . ." Sammy furrowed his brow.

I nodded. "Yep. You're named after him."

His eyes brightened. "Really? Do you think they call him Sammy?"

"I don't know."

Sammy smiled. "I bet I look just like him, then. I bet I do. Mom wouldn't have named me after him if I didn't, and she told us we have the same eyes."

"Maybe so, Sam."

He studied my face, as if he was making sure I wasn't playing a joke. "I never knew that. I didn't. Samuel."

I shrugged. "Come on. We'd better go." I pointed over the fields.

"You said he lived on Thirteenth. There's nothing but fields that way."

"It's not in Spokane. He lives in Walla Walla."

"Where's that?"

"South. Near the Oregon border."

"We're going to Oregon?"

"Close to it. Here, look." I held the map out to him and put my finger on Walla Walla, then on Spokane. I had no idea how long it would take to walk it, but on the map, it read one hundred and sixty miles, and that was by the highway. We couldn't walk on the highway. "Come on."

"Hey, Ian?"

"Yeah?"

"I'm sorry I kicked you. And called you that name."

"Don't worry about it, huh? I know you were mad."

"Like you were mad at your teacher?" Sam said.

"Sort of, I guess. It's okay, though." I hopped the fence and helped Sammy over, fixing our boards to our packs and heading toward the railroad line. With no trees, the sun beat on my head, and soon we were both sweating. Waist-high grass, dead from the year before, made walking over the lumpy pasture difficult, and when we reached the tracks, I unslung my pack and sat on a rail. Sammy joined me.

"Are we going to be like bums?"

"What?" I said absently, studying the map.

"Like bums. You know, on the railroad tracks."

I looked down the lines of metal for a moment, figuring the cops couldn't drive on them. "Yeah, I guess so. Like hobos."

"Cool. We should find sticks and tie red bags to the ends. Then we can be real hobos."

Before I could tell him we didn't have red bags, he was off looking for sticks. I returned to the map, figuring out where we were, but it didn't note railroad lines. I plotted a course I figured would take us in the general direction of Walla Walla, which might as well have been a million miles away.

Sammy came back empty-handed from the stick hunt, and we continued on. The track's timber was spaced so that walking over them fit me perfectly, but Sammy's legs were shorter, so he had to hop over the rock bed every once in a while to keep up. He chattered on about being hobos, and time flew by. He called it a grand adventure, like when we almost went to Seattle. We crested the first pine-covered hill I'd looked at from the fence, and it was the farthest I'd ever been from home.

I figured we'd gone several miles, and before I knew it, the sun hit the tops of the pines and the chill of dusk hit my cheek. It would be dark in an hour. Sammy slowed, both with the talking and the walking, and I was getting tired, too. We rested every once in a while on chunks of volcanic rock sticking from the sides of ravines, listening for trains.

"I'm thirsty."

"Me too," I said. The empty bottle of Mountain Dew had been sitting on the counter back home, but I hadn't thought of filling it with water and bringing it.

"And hungry."

I told Sammy we would find some water, and that we'd have the rest of the bread and doughnut for dinner.

"Are we sleeping outside?"

I nodded. "We'll find a place over the next hill—make a camp."

By the time we reached the hill, the pines were black against the fading blue of twilight. We hadn't found water, and Sammy was complaining, which was grating on my nerves. I snapped at him, and he shut up, taking on that whiny look again, and I knew he'd ask for Mom.

"I want Mom."

"I know. Me too. But we're here, and we'll make do, okay? It'll be fun. Like a campout." I didn't have a flashlight, and in a few minutes, it would be too dark to find a campsite. I led Sammy off the tracks, following a deer trail into the trees. I told him to pick up sticks as he went, and I did the same. Fifty yards into the trees, we came to a spot clear of underbrush.

I dropped my pile of wood, and Sammy followed suit. "We'll need more," I said. "Just don't go far."

Sammy looked around, the shadows deep under the trees. "I'm scared."

"We need a fire, Sam. You don't know how to make one, and I do. Just go around the clearing, huh? We'll be cold if I don't get this going." I set about gathering rocks for a fire ring, not giving him the chance to complain. A minute later, I heard him tromping along the edge of the clearing.

By the time I held the lighter to a bundle of pine needles, I could see my breath. Fifteen minutes later, I had a fire big enough to warm us, and Sammy had gathered wood to last awhile. My throat felt swollen, and I knew we were dehydrated, but I also knew you couldn't die from going without water for half a day. I brought out the rest of our food, which looked puny sitting on the blanket between us.

We ate dry bread and split the doughnut. We were still hungry, but it felt good to have something in my stomach. I knew that tomorrow we would have to do something about the food situation, and we also had to find water first thing. I hadn't peed in five hours, and figured we'd be in trouble by morning. I put another tree limb on the fire and searched for more wood, but I could hardly see in the dark. After ten minutes, I came back with a small bundle and put it on the pile, my fingers creaking with cold as I built up the fire.

The blanket we'd brought was from the army surplus, thick wool and scratchy. It was big enough for both of us and, I hoped, warm enough. I laid it out even, then told Sammy to get on it. We lay together and I flapped the edges over us, making a cocoon. I set the kitchen knife next to me.

Sammy moved closer to me. "Hey, Ian?"

"Yeah?"

"Call me Samuel from now on, okay?"

I didn't answer for a minute, thinking about our father. I'd never even seen a picture of him. He'd left so long ago that I didn't really have an image of him in my head. "You're Sammy."

"I want to be Samuel."

"You've never met him, Sam."

"He's prob'ly just like me. Mom wouldn't have named me after him if he wasn't."

"I don't know."

"Will you?"

"Let's wait till we meet him. Then you can decide. Fair?"

Sammy remained silent for a moment, watching his breath in the firelight. "Okay. But I want to be Samuel."

We lay for what seemed like forever, and I thought Sammy was asleep, but then he turned and propped himself up on his elbow. "I'm cold, Ian. This is dumb."

"It won't get under freezing tonight. It's spring. And besides, we can't go home."

"We could get closer to the fire, then."

"We'd catch on fire. Too dangerous." I slung my arm around him and pulled him close. "We can share heat. Two people are always warmer than one."

We stared into the flames. The wood crackled and spit, and

silence surrounded us. Shadows from the flames licked at the ring of trees surrounding our camp, and they reminded me of people running through the dark. I turned on my side, spooning against Sam, and felt his breathing.

"What if a bear eats us?" he whispered.

"It's okay. We're on a campout, remember? And I have the knife. I'll stab it."

"Think Mom's home?"

"No."

"You said she didn't want us anymore."

"She does, Sam, but she *is* sick, and sometimes she doesn't do what she's supposed to do."

"Then why'd you say it?"

"I don't know."

"I want her here. With us. I don't want her with that man anymore. He's scary."

"We're fine, Sam. Just stare in the fire. It makes you feel better." I pulled Sam closer, holding him tight, and we stared at the fire. If Mom were here, she'd probably be with the guy, and he would offer crack to Sammy or hit us or tell us to get the hell out. She would be high, too, and she wouldn't say anything when he did. She was a crack addict, I thought, and though I'd known it for a long time, I don't think I really ever accepted it. Here, with the fire in my eyes and my lids getting heavy, I did accept it, and the only thing I could ask God as I fell asleep was *why*.

I opened my eyes to a slim tendril of smoke rising from the fire ring. Frost covered the pines and a layer of white sparkled over the clearing. The blanket was crusted with it. I'd woken several

81

times during the night, shivering, and built up the fire, but we'd run out of wood several hours ago.

Sammy's eyes were open, staring at the sliver of smoke as he shivered, so I got up and gathered wood. Once I had the fire going, we stood by it, turning front to back, back to front, to warm ourselves. Sammy stomped his feet. "I got freaking freezing last night. Like an Eskimo." His voice sounded like a frog's, and I had an idea.

I walked over to the closest pine with low branches and snapped off a branch laden with needles. It glistened with frost. "Here." I handed a bunch to Sammy. "Stick the needles in your mouth and suck the frost off."

He didn't complain, but grabbed the white bundle and began. We went through two more branches before I could swallow without it feeling like my throat was made of sandpaper. I didn't even mind the sap.

"Good idea, Ian. Pinesicles."

My throat felt normal after a bit, but I knew it wouldn't be enough. "We still need water."

"We could go home. The cops are probably gone. Then we could have as much water as we wanted. Right out of the sink."

"We can't. They'll take us." I went down the list. Ms. Veer saw the pipe. They would say Mom is an unfit mother. I decked Coach Florence. Blah, blah, blah. I was so sick and tired of running through all the things we were up against that I vowed to not think about it again that day.

We packed up our stuff and stomped out the fire, returning to the rails. We hadn't seen a train yet, and I wondered if the rails were abandoned. Besides that, they seemed to be heading southwest, not south, and we needed south.

My legs ached from walking, and frozen ground hadn't exactly been the most comfortable place in the world to sleep, but after the first half hour of trudging, I loosened up. Sammy didn't say a word, just walked. No talk of hobos or grand adventures. We were hungry, and I had to find both food and water soon.

The tracks wound around the bigger hills, following low spots, and as we rounded a bend, Sammy spotted a deer and shouted. It threw its head up and stared, then bolted through the brush. I quickened my pace. "He was drinking, Sam. Hurry."

A rivulet bubbled from the hillside, following the tracks for several feet before soaking into the ground. Ice limned the edges. We fell to our knees and drank. The water froze my throat and filled my stomach. I'd had a headache since last night, and it ebbed as we sat, our bellies full of water, and watched the sun rise over the hill. Sammy patted his stomach. "That was the best water I've ever had. You could sell it, it's so good. It could be called Deer Water."

I read the map, but it was no use. I needed a landmark. A town or road or something. I guessed we were near a little town called Marshall, but I wasn't sure. "You probably could, Sammy. Hey, look." I showed him the map. "There's a town up here."

"Cops are in towns."

"Yeah, but there'll be houses. Like farms and ranches and stuff. Maybe we could get food."

"Like stealing a pie from a window?" he said.

I threw a pebble into the water and shook my head. "No. No stealing."

"Then how?"

"I don't know." We got up and walked for fifteen minutes, until a dirt road intersected the tracks, heading toward what I thought was the town. I looked for a road sign, but there was none. No intersections, either, just straight road. When the sun hit the trees, the frost melted, and soon the trees dripped. Little puffs of dust rose from our feet on the road.

Fifteen minutes later, we came to a driveway, and through the trees, a small house with a barn to the side sat in a clearing. I took Sammy up the drive, and as we neared, a man in his seventies walked from the barn. He wore rubber boots, overalls, and a tan cowboy hat. He held a pitchfork. When he saw us, he took his hat off and scratched his head, walking our way. "You boys lost?"

"No, sir."

He looked at the skateboards tied to our backpacks, then looked me up and down. "From the city?"

I nodded.

"What can I do for you?"

I looked where he'd come from and saw a big pile of hay. I pointed to it. "Can we do that for you?"

"You want work?" he said.

"Yes."

"Ain't got no money to pay."

"We don't need money."

He furrowed his brow, gripping the pitchfork tighter. "What, then?"

"Something to eat," I said. "Maybe a water bottle, a blanket, and a flashlight if you have enough for us to do."

"You boys run away?" He squinted.

"We're going to see our dad."

He smiled. "Traveling, huh?"

I nodded.

"I weren't born yesterday, son." He leaned on the pitchfork.

"I'm not lying," I said.

He chuckled. "Didn't say you were. Follow me."

His name was Dunbar Phillips, and he fried eggs for us while we sat at a rickety kitchen table. His wife had died five years before, and his kids were gone, a boy in Chicago and a girl in Seattle. He liked talking, and I enjoyed listening to him. I enjoyed even more the smell of melting butter and frying eggs, and Sammy was nearly drooling by the time the toaster popped and we ate.

He'd lived in the house since he'd bought it fifty-three years earlier, and he used to raise sheep for a living, shearing and selling. Now he kept a few cows and horses for company and bided his time until he would meet his wife again. I felt sorry for him. He kept talking, though, and we kept eating. He chuckled when Sammy asked for more, saying that he'd never had eggs so good.

After eating, he showed us outside and handed me the pitchfork. "There's another in the barn for your brother," he said, "and when you're done, I'll put you on something else if you care to."

Sammy and I pitched hay for an hour and a half, then shoveled horse and cow crap for another half hour, and I had blisters on my hands by the time we finished. Sammy worked hard and, after a few minutes of chattering, told me he'd like to live in a place like this. I told him he could if he set his mind to it, and he smiled. "Prob'ly gotta have good grades to get it, huh?" he said.

I laughed. "You got it, Sam." We were taking a fifteen-minute break, sitting on fence rails and rubbing our hands, when Mr. Phillips came from the house with a burlap sack. He set it down and told us we'd done a good job. Inside the sack, I found three cans of corn, a small jar of peanut butter, two cans of chili, and a loaf of bread. Under that was a blanket and a glass canning jar full of water.

"All I can spare, boys," he said. "Didn't have an extra flashlight or a canteen, but the jar should do."

I thanked him and told him we could work more, but he

waved us off, saying we'd done enough and that he didn't have any more to give. I was fine with that. My hands hurt like a son of a bitch, and Sammy was tired. We put our packs on, and I slung the sack over my back. We headed down the drive, waving as we went.

I was walking on air. No matter how tired we were, I thought it funny how good a sack of food could make a person feel. Things didn't seem so bad. We had an extra blanket and enough food for at least two days. I told Sammy I wanted to get a few more miles in for the day but that we'd camp early to rest. I pictured opening the can of chili and heating it in the saucepan over the fire, and my stomach growled. Early it would be.

Chapter Ten

Camp consisted of a rock overhang deep in a hollow somewhere in the middle of nowhere. We were lost. I'd wanted to
avoid the town, so we'd trekked cross-country for a mile or so,
hoping to hit another road or find the tracks. We didn't, and spent
the rest of the afternoon pushing on, straight south. I figured we'd
come across something marked on the map, but by the time the
sun lowered behind the trees, we hadn't found a thing.

Sammy tried to be brave, but when the night came, he snug-
gled next to me as tight as he could while I warmed the chili,
making me promise to keep the fire going all night. With the
extra blanket, I figured we'd stay warmer, and the saucepan in
my hand, the chili bubbling in it, made me feel in control. Like I
knew what I was doing. Tonight was no different from the night
before, really, I thought. We just didn't know where we were.

I tried to explain it to Sammy, but he still wanted the tracks.
He wanted home and asked for Mom before he fell asleep. With
the night around me and Sammy sleeping in my lap, I stared into
the fire. I'd screwed up. Coach Florence deserved to be punched,

but I shouldn't have done it. If I'd sucked up another humiliation and picked up the key like he'd asked, we wouldn't be here freezing our butts off like homeless people and running from the cops and CPS. None of it would have happened, I figured, if I wasn't who I was, and that thought sucked.

I laughed, thinking that we *were* homeless people and that I could feel sorry for myself forever, but it wouldn't change the fact that I was Ian and always would be. *I am what I am,* I thought, remembering Popeye the Sailor. I'd done what I'd done, and nothing could change it. I couldn't have ignored Florence. I'd rather have rotted in the woods.

The only problem was Sammy. He didn't deserve any of this, and I wondered if I was making the right decisions. Ms. Veer had talked about what was right and what was wrong, but I wasn't so sure. Then I thought about Coach Schmidt. The way she'd looked at me after I punched Florence surprised me: fear . . . but there was more. An understanding, maybe. Like she'd been in a similar circumstance and knew how it felt.

I wasn't stupid enough to think Coach Schmidt's life had been easy, and I realized that all the times she'd had me in her office, she hadn't talked about anything other than one thing. Respect. Even with the sports. Sure, she admitted she wanted a title, but everything else revolved around me. Not policy or rules or the right way to do things. She skated those issues, I realized, because she couldn't have gotten where she was without breaking a few rules herself. Respect. I knew then that she wouldn't have run.

I didn't realize I was contemplating going back until then, and I had to ask myself why. Reality was different from principles. Mom couldn't be a mom, Sammy was failing school, my school didn't even want me there, and the cops would be waiting. I put another stick in the fire and watched the flames take it over. We wouldn't go back. We'd make it to Walla Walla, and we'd find our father.

Dawn slid its way under my eyelids, and I took a second to remember where we were. Sammy slept soundly, the added blanket from Mr. Phillips making the difference. I'd stirred only two times during the night to feed the fire. I sneaked from the blanket and gathered wood, my toes and fingers freezing by the time I set the lighter to the tinder.

Our shoes were soaking wet from tramping through a bog the day before, and though we'd set them by the fire, they were still wet. I thought of the old pair of boots I hated wearing every winter and wished I had them, imagining warm toes and no moisture, no matter how ugly they were. Sammy had a pair, too, sitting beside mine in our closet, and I thought of all the things we should have packed and didn't.

I studied the map while Sammy slept and decided we'd come too far west because we'd missed the train tracks. We'd headed south, that I was sure of, but it couldn't have been straight south because we'd have intersected a gray slash that indicated a road. Our map sucked. It showed small roads but didn't give names. Once we did find a road, the only way to figure out where we were was to walk down it until we saw a sign with something more than a road name on it. Our map sucked, and I'd have to plot our course by towns.

Small towns dotted the byways. I wasn't too worried, but with our luck, we'd be going in circles for a week before realizing it. I also had the three bucks that Bennie had given me, and hoped we could find a store somewhere.

We'd head southeast today, or as near southeast as I could

figure, trying to find any landmark. I looked at the distance we'd come on the map, and it seemed puny. Good for two days' walking, but Walla Walla and the Oregon border, where the map ended, seemed a million miles away. It would take weeks.

Dejected, I opened a can of chili and put it in the pan, scraping coals to the side and setting it down. We'd eaten the other can last night, along with half the bread, but we still had the corn and some peanut butter, and for that I was glad.

By the time the chili bubbled, Sammy rubbed sleep from his eyes and stood. "The good thing about camping is that the bathroom is everywhere," he said, peeing from the edge of the blanket.

I laughed. "Come on and eat. We have to find a road today." I handed over the pan and watched him blow on a spoonful. We were dirty. Three days into it, and we hadn't washed so much as a finger. "We've got to clean up today. When we find water."

"Are we still lost?"

"No. I know right where we are."

"Where?"

"In the middle of nowhere."

Sammy smiled. "Ha, ha."

I ruffled his hair. "We'll find some more food today, too, okay?"

"Are we out?"

"Almost. We don't have any water, either, so don't ask."

Sammy spooned the last of the chili into his mouth. "I'm gonna have farts." He held up two fingers. "Chili last night and chili now. Beans, beans, the magical fruit. The more you eat, the more you toot."

We packed up our stuff and headed southeast, or what I

thought was southeast. An hour later, we hadn't come across anything, but as we topped a rise, I saw a farmhouse in the distance, which meant a road.

Our legs were wet from the knees down from the dew coating the fields, and my feet steamed in the sun when we rested, warming my toes. Twenty minutes later, with the farmhouse within shouting distance, we rested on a small knoll, looking at the house. White with green trim, it had peaked roofs and a porch running around the entire front. Several outbuildings and a white barn dotted the property, and we had to climb a barbed-wire fence with a NO TRESPASSING sign to reach the road. Sammy ripped his jeans on it and snagged himself; his leg ran blood to his shoe, and he cried.

I helped him to the road and knelt next to him, pressing my extra shirt against the cut until it stopped bleeding. The screen door on the house banged, and a woman in her fifties with gray hair pulled back in a braid walked onto the porch and stared at us. After a moment, she put her hands on her hips and raised her chin. "What're you boys doing out there?"

I stood, pointing down the road. "Is there a town that way?"

"Malden. Are you boys lost?"

I helped Sammy to his feet, and we walked, avoiding any more questions. Once the house was out of sight, we sat on the shoulder of the road. A robin lit on the fence across from us, its tail seesawing to keep its balance. Malden. I thought we were on Wells Road, traveling south, but I wasn't sure. Each one-inch square on the map equaled twenty miles. Frustrated, I put the map in my pocket. "Malden is around ten miles away. How's your leg?"

"It stings."

"You'll be fine. It's not bleeding anymore, is it?"

"No," he said, rolling his eyes dramatically, "but it's prob'ly broken."

I smirked. "Looks like we'll have to cut it off, then."

His eyes widened.

"I'm joking."

He frowned, then rubbed his belly. "I'm hungry."

"It's still morning. We'll eat later."

"But I'm hungry, Ian. And I'm tired of walking. We walk and walk and that's all we do. When are we going to be there?"

"Walla Walla?"

He nodded.

"I don't know. A long time, I think."

"You could use the cell phone."

"For what? A taxi?"

"No. Call that lady. Ms. Veer. She could give us a ride."

"No."

"Why?"

"Because we're fine." Once again I was tempted to throw the stupid thing away, but I didn't. Whether that was because it was nice and expensive and had a flip thing on it or because I thought I *might* use it, I didn't know. But it stayed in my pack.

Sammy sprawled out on the ground like some delusional madman reeling from starvation, then rolled onto his belly, looking at me. "We're starving to death, and I think my leg is broken."

"We're hungry, and your leg isn't broken. Don't be a wuss, Sam. We're on an adventure, remember?" I dug in my pack and took the peanut butter out, handing it to him.

He unscrewed the lid and gouged out a chunk with his finger, sticking it in his mouth and sucking. I figured the dirt on his fingers was a decent seasoning. He licked his chops and stuck his finger in again. "I could read a book and be in an adventure. That's what my teacher always says, and you don't have to be hungry and break your leg when you're sitting at home with a book. I'm sick of this adventure." He showed me his peanut butter–covered finger. "Can I have bread with this?"

I shook my head no. "So now you like school, then, Mr. Reader?" I smiled.

He laid his cheek down on the ground. "Yeah. Better than walking a billion miles with a broken leg and pretending my finger is bread."

I stood, holding my hand out for the jar. "Come on. We have to walk because we're in the middle of nowhere and we *do* need to get food. And besides, that old lady probably called the cops."

He looked at me. "You're not fooling about Dad? He's real?"

"I'm not fooling, Sam."

"Samuel."

"Come on, then, Samuel." I kept track of the sun moving across the sky, and I figured three hours went by before we came within sight of the town, which was near an intersection of the road on the map. Directly east was Highway 195, and I was tempted to intersect it. The highway would be a straight shot down, and maybe we could hitch a ride. But we hadn't seen a single soul. No cars, no farmers in the fields, no nothing. The back roads were safest. Nothing but endless rolling crops and hollows filled with pines. "We're going about three miles an hour."

Sammy slid his feet, kicking up dust. "Yippee. We can't even ride our boards 'cause of the dirt."

"That's pretty good, I think." We were near Malden, and when we passed the intersection sign telling us Malden was east and Pine City was south, we walked south.

93

We walked to and through Pine City, which I figured had to be the smallest city in the world, smaller than the smallest town I'd ever seen. I set my sights on St. John, which was on Highway 23. Another gray road led south from there, to Endicott, then ran into Highway 26 at a place called Dusty, which looked to be around halfway to Walla Walla.

Sammy polished off most of the peanut butter and three slices of bread by late afternoon, and I knew we wouldn't reach St. John by dark. We stopped at a culvert on the side of the road and washed up, filling our jar and resting for a half hour. Sammy leaned back and stared at the sky. "What do you think he's like?"

I pulled a shoot of grass from the ground, peeling off the end and sticking it in my mouth like Tom Sawyer. I never knew so much farmland surrounded Spokane. It seemed endless. "I don't know. Probably a normal kind of guy."

"You think he has a house? Like a real one that he owns?"

"Maybe. Maybe a job, too." *And maybe a whole other family,* I thought.

"I bet he's rich." Sammy raised his arms and made a triangle with his fingers, looking through it at a cloud drifting by.

I threw the stem away. "Maybe so, Sam." I smiled, letting his enthusiasm take my own imagination on a trip. "With a pool. That'd be nice, too. A pool with a diving board." I pictured having my own room filled with all the things regular kids had. Computers and TVs and a DVD collection and an awesome stereo lined themselves up in my head, and I smiled. Maybe I could even have my own cell phone. One that I could actually call somebody on, instead of the one in my pack. With that thought, I dug for it and turned the power off. I had no idea how long it would last, but if we really got in trouble, I wanted some juice left in it.

Sammy kept talking. "And he could take us to school every day and we'd have lunch 'cause he'd go in the office and pay for it. That way the lunch ringer-upper lady wouldn't look at me that way. That'd be sooooo cool."

"It would."

"And maybe he would let Mom live with us, huh?" Sammy sat up, looking at me, excitement in his eyes. "Yeah, he could do that, couldn't he? He could go get her, and when she saw him in his nice car and with his hair all combed and maybe a flower or something in his hand, she'd leave that place with the guy you beat up."

The thought of that made my new fantasy room turn back to my old one. The one with the sunken bed and broken dresser. "Sure, Sam."

"And then they'd be together, and he could make sure she did all the right things, huh? She wouldn't leave or nothing. Just stay home and stuff."

I stared at the ground between my knees. *No, Sam,* I thought. *That won't happen.* He left for a reason, and I wondered if it was us or her. Maybe both. "Sure, Sam. He could probably do that." I stood. "Let's go."

Chapter Eleven

My belly clawed at my insides like a crazy monkey trying to scratch its way out, and Sammy complained over and over again about being hungry. I looked at him, and he *did* look skinnier. My own pants were loose around my waist. Three days of walking and not eating enough did that to a person, I thought, and although we might not be near starvation, hunger was taking a toll.

We hiked away from the road just before dark, with no sign of St. John in the distance. I'd noticed that the towns were built in small valleys. Green and usually with a creek running through them, they surprised you as you topped a rise or hill. For all I knew, we could be a quarter mile from it. Camp consisted of eating the rest of the food—corn and peanut butter—and sleeping under a batch of trees in another hollow.

I'd thought about stopping at the tiny store in Pine City to use the money in my pocket but decided, to my regret, that I should save it for really bad times. I didn't make a fire. We were too tired. Just ate and fell asleep. Sammy didn't ask for Mom.

• • •

The sun came up, and our packs didn't have an ounce of anything edible in them. I dearly wished for another Dunbar Phillips to come along, but we couldn't risk running into another lady who might call the police, so we walked.

Back on the road, I looked to the horizon and clouds, thick and gunmetal, gathered like an army of cops and judges and state workers coming after us. To the west, rain—streams of dark lines reaching the ground—hit the fields, and I knew we were in for it. But we couldn't find shelter without food, and another twelve hours of walking without something to eat wasn't an option. My legs were rubber and my whole body ached, and I wondered if a person knew he was starving to death before he really was.

We walked for three hours, parallel to the clouds coming from the west, and the rain approached. I could smell it. Lightning streaked here and there. The wind picked up, cold and harsh. No driveways. Nothing. I thought St. John would be closer than it was, and we were heading straight for those bad times I'd thought about when we'd gone through Pine City. "Shit."

"It's gonna rain." Sammy shivered.

"I know." Spring storms in eastern Washington could be the coldest, nastiest sleet- and hail-filled nightmares imaginable. I'd been caught in a few, and even if it was seventy degrees in front of the clouds, it could be forty, even thirty, inside them.

Twenty minutes later, the first raindrop, big and heavy and cold, hit my hand. The wind against my face bit hard. Five minutes later, the sky spit on our heads, and five minutes after that, I was digging in our packs for every bit of clothing we had. I took the blankets and handed one to Sammy, helping him wrap it around his shoulders. We put our knit skullcaps on and pulled them low. Sammy's teeth chattered. "We should stop, Ian. It's really starting now." He looked up and opened his mouth, catching a drop or two on his tongue. Thunder rolled across the fields deep and hollow, and as I looked across to the horizon, I saw nothing but stinking fields.

"No. We keep walking."

"I'm cold, Ian. Please."

"No, Sam. We walk. It'll keep us warmer."

"I can't walk. My legs won't go anymore." Tears came to his eyes.

"Yes, you can. We're tough. Like that wrestler guy you like. Stone Cold Steve Austin, right? Come on. We can either sit and be freezing or walk, but if we sit, we get no food at least until tomorrow."

"We could go under some trees or something. I saw an Indian eat bark once, too. We could eat bark and ants and make a teepee."

"We'll find something, okay? Just keep going, Sam. It'll be fine." We trudged on, the rain getting worse.

"I want Mom, Ian." He cried harder, his chest heaving, his teeth chattering. His lips were turning blue, and water streamed down his face.

"I know."

"I want her now!" He stomped his foot, hugging the blanket closer and putting his chin against his chest. "I don't care if she doesn't do things right, and I don't care about anything! *I want Mom, and I don't want to be here anymore!*"

Tears came to my eyes now, and I hated them. I hated this feeling in me like an ache so deep, and I hated even more that it was telling me I was in over my head. It had been more than forty-eight hours since we'd eaten a full meal, breakfast at Mr. Phillips's ranch, and we'd hiked for more than twenty of those hours. I knew what was happening. We were exhausted. My muscles ached, and my eyes just wanted to close and wake up a year from now with a big table of food in front of me. But we couldn't have it. There was no could or wish or want or anything out here. There was only freezing rain, endless nothing from one hill to the next, and darkness. "We have to walk. I told you we'd find something, and we will, but you have to keep going! Trust me, Sammy, we can do this."

He cried harder, catching his breath even as the rain pounded down on us. Lightning flashed, and a few seconds later, thunder rattled my teeth. Huge, bone-jarring thunder. I took Sammy by the shoulder and hugged him, urging him down the road. Twenty minutes later, we were soaked and frozen to the bone, with no sign of the rain letting up. An hour later, the road became a mush of mud, caking our shoes and sucking at our feet. I couldn't feel my toes. My nose ran and my stomach hurt and my legs were Jell-O, and there wasn't a point to anything in this whole rotten, soggy, crappy world.

Sammy fell down twice in the next two hours, complaining he was dizzy, then said he had to go to the bathroom, so we stopped and he scampered over an embankment. I stood because I couldn't sit unless I wanted to sink into inches of mud, and shivers racked my entire body. I figured it was about five in the afternoon. Then I saw headlights.

In every movie I'd ever seen, this is where the kindly old man in a beat-up truck would stop and take in the fugitive kids, feeding them and building a big fire in the hearth. His floppy-eared dog would lick their hands, and they'd drink hot chocolate and listen to stories of storms fifty years ago. I waited, too tired to join Sammy and hide until it passed, and through the rain, I watched as the vehicle splashed closer. As luck would have it, the kindly old man was replaced by a man in a cowboy hat, and the truck was replaced by a car with a rack of lights and SHERIFF blazed along the sides.

This was it, I thought. There'd be no explaining our way out of this mess. The only reason two idiots would be out in the middle of nowhere in the midst of a huge storm would be to run from something, and the sheriff would know in a heartbeat what to do when he saw a skater punk standing on a muddy road like a lost fugitive. I wondered if he had two pairs of handcuffs.

He slowed his approach and pulled to the side, stopping in front of me. His headlights blared into my eyes, so I looked away, toward the embankment where Sammy had gone. The door opened and he got out, plastic wrapped around his cowboy hat. He wore a green slicker with SHERIFF printed in yellow over his breast, and he hitched up his belt before walking to me.

I'd figure a man with a warm car waiting would be in a hurry to get back in it, but he stopped in front of me, the headlights casting a long-legged shadow past me, and studied me. "You look downright miserable, boy."

I stared at him. His eyes stayed on mine, but I didn't really notice them. I noticed the raindrops splashing from the plastic-coated brim of his cowboy hat. It rained so hard that they made a fuzzy halo around his head. I looked to his waist, saw the belt leading to the pistol covered by the slicker, and wondered if he'd ever used it.

The painted-on star over the left breast of the slicker was nearly level with my eyes. The guy was tall, a skinny six feet six, and had no meat to back up his height. I knew he had pepper spray and a baton dangling opposite the hidden pistol. He should have been a basketball player, not a scarecrow sheriff in a rain-proof cowboy hat.

I was at a loss. I didn't realize how miserable I was until he said it. Tired, hungry, weak, shaky, and desperate to make the blue leave my brother's lips. My mind raced, but it felt like the sucking mud of the road filled my brain. What I did see was our future. The tall sheriff in front of me held it, and I could see it clear as the blue sky behind the sheet of clouds dumping on us. In the car, to the station. Phone calls. Then we'd be taken back. I'd go to juvie; Sammy would go to a state home. The sheriff held it all.

On the other hand, I saw a warm car, a dry station house, hot food, and Sammy sleeping on a mattress. I saw Mom trying the best she could to make appointments on time, pleading my case, pleading her case, and jumping through hoops that people like her had no chance of clearing. I also saw a man in a black robe who didn't know us deciding what was best for us. I saw it all, and the only thing I wanted was to shrivel up into a muddy ball and disappear.

"You're in a sorry mess, boy, and I can't help you unless you talk," he said, looking me up and down. Water ran in rivulets from the ends of the blanket around my shoulders, and I couldn't stop shaking. Sammy hadn't come back yet. "You going to tell me a story?"

"What do you want to hear?" I said dejectedly, raising my voice over the roar of the rain.

"The truth."

"We're going to see our dad."

"We?" he said, backing up a step and looking around. His hand went to his side.

I nodded.

"Who's we?"

I saw it coming and didn't do anything. It had to be a soggy mirage or delusion from not eating or just my imagination. Sammy came over the embankment from behind and to the side of the sheriff. He carried a broken fence post as thick as my wrist. He came like a cat, and the look in his eyes held something dead and emotionless that scared me as he wound back and swung.

I couldn't stop it. I didn't try to stop it. The waterlogged post caught the officer squarely on the side of his knee, and even with the rain drumming around us, I heard the crunch of the joint buckling. The sheriff's feet went out from under him, and he went down, crumpled and holding his ruined knee.

As he screamed and rocked back and forth in the mud, his eyes locked on mine in an instant, and I could see his thoughts. This had gone from him talking to a runaway kid in a downpour to a life-threatening situation. His hand went for his holster.

I jumped forward, screaming at him to stop, and my hand reached his belt just as he unsnapped the holster. I was faster. I grabbed the handle and yanked, ripping it from the leather and spinning away from him. He tried to rise, but his ruined knee buckled. He lay back, his eyes flicking from the gun in my hand and riveting on my face. Then I saw it. The look. The same that I'd seen in Coach Schmidt's eyes after I'd hit Florence. Fear.

I held the pistol. Finally, I had control over everything. I could point it at him and pull the trigger, and I could be the person they thought I was. The weight of the pistol bore down on me, and the cold steel fit like a glove in my clenched fist, sent a shudder up my arm. I grimaced. I wasn't that person.

I wound back and threw it, and as I watched it lose shape through the rain, some of that confusion about what I was sailed away with it. I might be bad, but I wasn't what they thought.

Relief flooded the sheriff's face when I turned back to him, and something clicked between us, an understanding of what was happening here. His voice was low and clear over the pelting rain. "I don't know what the problem is, son, but I'm not here to hurt you."

Water streamed down my face. I didn't know what to do, but I couldn't end this. Not the way my body, exhausted and beaten down, wished for. I nodded. "I know."

He glanced at Sammy, then back to me. "Then we can figure this out."

"You don't understand."

He stared at me for another moment, then nodded. "I know I don't. But it's not worth it. It's never worth it."

I sniffed, my breath still coming hard. I knew what he was. He wasn't bad or out to get us or anything else. He was just a guy lying in the mud with a busted-up knee, and like me, he wanted this to be over. I'd never felt so lost before, and for the first time in a long time, I wished my dad, the one I'd imagined and the one who hadn't left us, was here. I looked at him again. "You have kids?"

He nodded slowly.

The rain fell. "What would you tell them to do?"

Steam streamed from his mouth. "I'd tell them to work things out. To do the right thing."

I blinked, wishing I could, but knowing the right thing for them might not be the right thing for us. "I can't. Not now."

"Don't make that mistake, son. You can."

The rain pounding my shoulders felt like the entire world telling me there was no hope. I nodded toward Sammy. "The only thing I have is him, and you'll take him." I took a breath. "I can't let that happen." I called to Sammy, "Open the door, get his keys, and unplug the radio microphone. Hurry." I looked at the sheriff while Sammy did what he was told. "Can you stand?"

"I don't know."

"Try." I wanted to help him up, but I couldn't allow him to get close. He struggled and grunted in pain, went back down on one knee, but finally made it upright. He lurched over to the hood of the car, barely able to keep on his feet. Sammy came around with the keys and handset, the unplugged cord bouncing and dangling as he hurried. He handed them to me, the keys cold and wet in my hand. I stuffed the handset in my pack pocket, then looked across the fields for a second. "I'll leave your keys in the fields. Follow our footsteps in the mud and you'll find them." I glanced at his knee. "Not too far, just enough to give us some time."

He leaned against the car. "You don't have to do this."

I backed away. "I'm sorry about your knee. It shouldn't have happened this way." He started to say something, but I cut him off. "I can't do it your way. I'm sorry."

Then we were gone, over the embankment and in the fields. I don't know how long we ran, really, and I have no idea *how* we did it, but we did. In some places the mud reached over my ankles, and the rain beat down so hard it hurt. I set the keys down on a rock when I thought we were far enough away, but I kept the handset, figuring his disabled radio would give us more time.

As I set the keys down, I put my hands on my knees and tried to catch my breath. I glanced over at Sammy, who stood a few feet away, watching me. He said nothing, and I wanted it that way. He'd scared me. Not just what he did, but how he did it. Those eyes. So dead and emotionless when I saw him swing the post. I wondered if I looked that way when I hit Florence.

● ● ●

We didn't speak. Sammy trudged and ran and stumbled along beside me, and after a while, I realized he was crying. Once, he doubled over and vomited. I waited until he wiped his mouth, then continued.

We slogged over hills and through ravines, and after a while, I saw a house. I knew we were in trouble. Bigger trouble than ever, and we had to get out of this county. Out of this world. If Sammy fell one more time and couldn't get back up, I wouldn't have the strength to carry him.

It wasn't fully dark yet, but the clouds made it dusky, and the rain made it hard to see. The porch lights were on, and light streamed through closed blinds. I hoped nobody would be fool enough to be outside on an evening like this, because I was at the point where I'd do anything to get out of this situation.

The rain blurred my vision, and the sound of the raindrops slamming into the tin roof of the barn off to the side of the house deafened me. We circled around, coming at the barn from the side away from the house, and I found a side door next to a chicken coop. The second we stepped inside the dim, hay-smelling place, I felt better.

It reminded me of Dunbar Phillips's barn. Two-by-four stalls, tools mounted along one wall, sacks of feed, and piles of hay. I ducked around two sets of tack hung from a beam. "Take the blanket off and hang it over a rail, Sam." He did so, shivering uncontrollably as water ran down his face.

Set in the middle of the barn and facing the double doors leading out was an old pickup truck. I slung my own blanket over a rail and tried the rusty door, opening it and hopping in the driver's seat. I searched the cab for keys, hoping they kept them in the visor or under the seat, but came up empty-handed. We needed heat, and if I could start it, we'd be warm. Then I looked at the ignition. A screwdriver was jammed in it. Sammy peeked through the window, and I told him to hop in, so he trudged around and opened the passenger-side door.

I twisted the screwdriver, and it clicked, the engine firing as I pumped the gas. The rain pounded on the barn roof like a thousand feet rattling on aluminum grandstands, and I wasn't worried about anybody hearing the engine over the clatter. I turned the heater on, hopped out, opened the side door of the barn for the exhaust, and grabbed our blankets. Back inside, I shut the creaky driver-side door and set the blankets on the floorboards to dry, which would probably take about eight years.

Sammy and I sat silent for five minutes, shivering and squeezing our arms together before the engine warmed up and the heater blew hot air. Sammy huddled down near the floor, curling up and holding his fingers together near the vent, and I put my hands to the upper vent. Soon the windows fogged up and we steamed like pavement after a summer rain.

I told Sam to take off his shoes and socks, and I did the same, putting them next to the floor vents. I knew it would take hours, if not all night, for our shoes to dry, and the rain still beat a steady drum on the barn roof. But we weren't freezing. We couldn't go back out in it, I knew, and we couldn't risk staying, either. But we were warming up, the rain wasn't pounding us, and Sammy's lips weren't so blue. "We've got to go, Sam."

He shook his head no.

I nodded. "We'll take the pickup. Borrow it and leave it just like we found it, just somewhere else."

He nodded, looking up at me from the floor. "I'm dizzy, Ian, and I feel all weird inside. Like I have to throw up but can't." He hadn't said more than two words since hitting the sheriff, and I didn't want to deal with that issue anyway. I hopped from the cab and walked outside, the rain sending an instant shudder through me as I slogged to the chicken coop, my knife in my hand.

The biggest thing I'd ever killed before had been a mouse in the kitchen, and my stomach squirmed a little bit as I scanned the coop for the easiest targets. I didn't know if chickens bit people, but we needed food, and if I'd learned anything in the last few days, it was that you'd kill anything if you were hungry enough.

After a scramble around the coop, I caught a big hen and held it by its neck, the bird clawing and pecking at my hands and arm. Then it quieted. I'd seen some show on TV where this lady in Alabama or something killed a chicken, and she'd chopped its head off with a cleaver. I walked out of the coop with it, held the bird down on the concrete entry, and chopped with the knife. The head came off easier than I figured. It stopped moving after a moment, so I went and caught another one, repeating what I'd done with the first one.

Sammy's eyes widened when he saw the headless birds in my hands and widened further when he saw the blood on my fingers, so I stuffed the carcasses behind the seat and wiped my hands on a blanket. I got out and walked to the double doors, peeking out to see if anybody was there. All clear.

I'd driven my mother's car around the block one time before she'd sold it, and another time I'd driven Blind Man Thompson down to the store, but I'd never driven an old truck through the mud in a downpour. But I could do it. I had to do it.

The blinds were closed in the house, and I hoped we could sneak by without being seen. I swung the doors wide, then bolted for the truck, hopping in and putting it in drive. It lurched forward until I found the brake, then I gave it some gas with my other foot and it crept forward.

When the rain hit the windshield, I had a moment of panic, trying to find the windshield-wiper knob and fumbling with the headlights, turning them on by accident. I held my breath, hoping that no one in the house had seen the flash, then found the wipers. I turned them on high and didn't wait a second longer, giving the truck more gas. Then we were out, slogging down the drive at what seemed a snail's pace.

Chapter Twelve

figured the safest bet would be three hours in the truck before we left it somewhere or ran out of gas. Any longer than that and we'd be caught, with either the owner reporting it stolen or chance bringing another policeman our way. I thought we were headed south but had no idea what road we were on. We'd run several miles over the fields, and from my map I could guess, but wasn't sure. We'd have to come to a town sooner or later, though, and then I'd know what direction to take.

Sammy kept looking behind the seat at the dead chickens, and after the third time, asked me if I knew how to cook them. "I suppose pluck the feathers, cut it, and scoop the guts out," I replied, distracted by the weather and the mud and the awkward steering. I didn't trust myself to go much faster than thirty miles an hour, and every once in a while the mud under the tires gave way, sending us sliding and also sending my heart into my throat.

Thirty was better than three, though, and I decided to never take traveling by automobile for granted again. But the truck made me nervous. It would be a way to find us, and I knew that once the sheriff got to a phone, there'd be a major search underway. I stepped up our speed, and over the rolling and rain-battered hills we went. An hour later, our clothes were dry except for our butts and any creases in the fabric, and we had the cab boiling hot. Sammy yawned a few times, and when I glanced over the last time, he'd closed his eyes.

Curled up in a ball on the floor, he looked small. Not big enough to do what he had to the sheriff, that's for sure, and I wondered what was wrong with him. I remembered that look while it happened, and it was like there wasn't anything there. Like he'd just chopped another log in a big pile of logs to chop.

I'd seen him that way once or twice before, and I was smart enough to realize he did stuff like that when things went bad for us. When he was under stress. I imagined him getting into that fight at school where he'd busted the kid's lip, and I knew he'd had that look in his eyes. It was like he stepped out of himself and stopped feeling things. I wondered again if Mom had been addicted when Sammy was born, and wondered if I'd made the right choices. Maybe he needed more than me. Maybe he needed people who knew more, people who knew how to handle him.

I didn't want to ask him if he felt bad for hitting the sheriff, because I was afraid I wouldn't like the answer. Sammy didn't understand the differences between things sometimes, and sometimes he didn't feel things like I thought he should.

As I drove, I thought about that. I'd socked Coach Florence and shouldn't have. Whether or not he deserved it, or even whether Malachi did for that matter, didn't make a difference. But there was a difference in the way *I* felt about things like that and the way my brother did.

I understood Sammy well enough to see his thinking. The sheriff would have taken us, but Sammy didn't know the boundaries, and I was beginning to think there might not be any for him. He was turning into me, I realized, but Sammy was different. His brain worked differently, and it had to do with the drugs.

"You're mad at me."

I looked down, and Sammy stared at me. "I'm not mad, Sam."

"Yes, you are. Ever since I hit that guy."

"I was scared. I thought he would shoot us."

Sammy burrowed his chin into his chest, looking at his fingers.

I slowed for a curve and noticed the rain had let up a bit. "I don't think you should have done what you did, Sammy." I remembered the sickening sound of the sheriff's knee buckling.

"You do it."

"It's not the same."

"Why?"

"He didn't deserve it, Sam. He was just doing his job. Just like the security guard downtown. He wasn't trying to hurt us."

"You said foster homes had bad stuff happen. And you would go to jail, too. Prob'ly forever."

"Yeah, I would, but not forever. But you can't go around hurting people like that."

"I didn't mean to hurt him, Ian. I didn't. I just hit him so he wouldn't bug us."

I stared down the road. "Okay."

"You sure?"

"Yeah, I'm sure." I looked over at him, not sure of anything. "I love you, Sam."

He smiled, burrowing deeper under the dash. "Love you, too. Mom, too. Don't forget her."

I nodded.

He was silent for a moment. "Say you love her."

I glanced at him, then stared out the windshield. "I love her."

Twenty minutes after the rain stopped, we stopped. Actually, we ran out of gas, which was just as well because I was having a hard time focusing on the road. We'd gone through a town called Winona. I'd found our bearings on the map, then driven on to a place called Lacrosse, which was near Highway 26. We drove on 26 for a little bit, then headed south on a back road toward a town called Hay, where we ran out of gas three miles outside the town limits.

By the map, I figured we'd come more than sixty miles in the truck, and only when we stopped did I think of the odometer. Oh well. But sixty miles took us out of the county we'd been in, and sixty miles was four days of walking. The map noted Central Ferry State Park a bit down the road, so we grabbed our still-damp blankets, tied the chickens to my pack, and headed toward it. We were close.

The sun had long gone down and it was pitch-black, but after we'd walked an hour, the clouds broke and a few stars replaced the clouds. I didn't care to see another raindrop for the rest of my life. We'd be cold tonight in those damp blankets, but if it didn't rain, I figured a big fire and roasted chicken would keep us alive. We found the park through the starlight and headed off to the side, finding a secluded spot near a boulder with an overhang. Sammy was dragging big-time and wouldn't talk. Underneath the overhang I found dry twigs, so I gathered them and then searched for the driest wood I could find, digging under brush and rotted logs, and brought them back to camp. Sammy was too tired to do anything but sit and stare at me.

It took a half hour to start the fire, but once I had it going, I piled wood around the edges to dry. My hands shook so badly that plucking and gutting the chickens was almost impossible, but the good thing was that I was so hungry and exhausted I didn't get grossed out as the slime of the guts coated my fingers. After cutting off the legs, I had Sammy hold them over the fire by the claws while I cut chunks of breast meat and put them on a sharpened stick.

Soon the smell of chicken fat dripping in the fire had both of us staring at the meat like it was sent from heaven. I made Sammy wait until it was done, then we ripped into it, burning our lips on the grease and not caring a bit about it. We feasted, eating the first chicken down to the bones, me all the while telling Sam to slow down or he'd get sick, and then snacking on part of the second chicken until we were stuffed.

After tucking the last of the roasted chicken meat in a shirt and packing it away, I stood by the fire with Sammy, the still-damp blankets around us, turning circles as they steamed themselves dry. Bone tired, my body wouldn't cooperate with me, and I almost fell into the fire twice before I took Sammy's blanket and laid it down. He fell on it, and after putting the second blanket over him, I moved the wood away from the fire, built the flames high, and curled up next to him.

Chapter Thirteen

*T*he sun broke under a clear sky, thank God, and I woke with the first streams of light piercing through my eyelids. The fire was stone-cold dead; I hadn't risen to stoke it because I'd been so tired. I opened my eyes, thinking of the sheriff and hoping he was all right. Every muscle in my body screamed as I piled sticks and set the lighter to them. Sammy could have been a log, he slept so soundly. I rubbed my hands over the tiny flames licking up, the smoke curling through my fingers and warming them. I figured that by the end of this trip, I'd be able to build a fire at the bottom of a lake.

I had to go to the bathroom, so I walked away from camp, and when I came back, I saw a man standing at the edge of the clearing, staring at Sammy curled up in the blankets. I stopped, not wanting to draw attention to myself, as shivers ran up my spine.

Fully bearded, he looked around twenty-five or so. He had a bedroll and an old backpack, wore dirty jeans and a hooded sweatshirt, and stood as quiet and still as a cat staring at a mouse. I didn't know if he was trouble, but the knife lay next to the blanket, and I was a good twenty feet from it. He was closer than I was.

114

The fire curled a wisp of smoke up its own invisible chimney. Sammy lay still. The man hadn't seen me because he was so intent on the scene, and when I stepped forward, his eyes shot up and narrowed. I ignored him, pretending I hadn't seen him as I walked as quickly as I could toward the fire, my eyes on the knife. When I reached it, I kicked Sammy's leg and bent down, gathering wood and putting it on the fire, my hand inches from the weapon.

On one knee and with the knife at my fingertips, I raised my eyes to him, and we stared at each other for a moment. Then he turned and disappeared into the brush. My heart beat in my throat and my hands were sweaty as I jostled Sammy. "Wake up, Sam, we've got to go. Wake up."

Sammy didn't stir.

I put my hands on his shoulders and shook him, glancing back at where the man had been. Sammy groaned, and when he did, his breath, hotter than it should have been, hit my face. I felt his forehead. It was burning up, but he wasn't sweating. "Sammy, please, wake up. Wake up, Sam."

He groaned again and opened his eyes, barely slits against the sunshine streaming down. "Achy," he said, then closed his eyes.

"Wake up, Sam. Come on. Tell me what's wrong."

Sam opened his eyes again, then turned on his side. "I don't feel so good, Ian. Real bad. Achy and stuff, and my head hurts a lot," he whispered.

"He's sick."

I spun around, the knife in my hand, and faced the stranger. He stood next to the fire staring at us, his bedroll hanging from his backpack, his boots muddy. I stood, pointing the knife at him. "What do you want?"

He shook his head, then gestured to Sammy. "He needs help."

"Why did you leave?"

"You were scared," he said, then knelt by the fire. "I coulda done you harm before you woke."

I took a breath. "I don't know that, and I don't know you. Leave."

He looked at Sammy curled up. "Get the blanket off him. He's got a fever."

"I said leave."

He fed a stick into the fire. "You don't know what the hell to do, do you?" He smiled, shaking his head.

I shifted back to Sammy, bending down and throwing the blanket from him. He groaned but kept his eyes shut. "If you try anything, I'll stab you. I swear."

"There's no doctor around here."

"Are you a doctor?" I said, looking him up and down.

He shook his head. "No, but I can help him."

"How?"

"Because I've been sick on the road just like him." He dug in his pack. "And I've got these." He held up an orange bottle of pills.

"What are they?" I said, not lowering the knife.

"They take the fever away. Won't make him better all at once, but if that fever gets too high . . ."

"I don't believe you. They could be anything."

He nodded. "You're right. But I guess you gotta decide what you trust more. Me or that fever going away on its own."

I glanced at Sammy, and he moved, thrashing in slow motion and feeling for the blanket I'd taken away. "I'll kill you if you hurt him."

He smiled. "With that look in your eyes, I bet you could. You've seen some bad shit, haven't you?"

I shrugged.

He looked at our skateboards, then at me. "City punk caught in a rough spot, huh?" He popped the top on the bottle. "You got water?"

I moved over to my pack, keeping him in front of me. I took out the jar of water.

"Good. You'll need more. Lots more. Gotta flush his system. Give me your knife."

I shook my head.

"He can't have a whole pill. He's too small. I've got to cut it in half."

"Give me the pill, and I'll do it."

He tossed the pill over the fire and I caught it.

"Half will do for now. The other half in four hours. Cut it on that rock by you."

I knelt and cut the pill as carefully as I could. "He can't take pills. He chokes."

"Crush it and mix it in the water."

I did so, then helped Sammy to sit. "Drink, Sam. There's medicine in it. Come on." Sammy barely opened his eyes, and when he drank, he made a face like he'd vomit. "Don't throw up, Sam. Come on. Keep it down."

He did, and after the last was gone, he started crying, telling me he wanted Mom. "You're okay, Sam. It's fine. You'll feel better in no time." His body was burning up. I laid him back down and felt his forehead, which was hotter than before.

I studied him for a moment, hoping I was doing the right thing, and anger boiled up in me. I clenched my teeth. I felt helpless, and just like Sammy, I wished Mom was here. She would know what to do. The stranger sat cross-legged and looked at me. I still held the knife and didn't plan on letting it go any time soon. "You think he'll be all right?"

He shrugged. "I don't know. My name is Craig."

"Ian. That's Sammy."

"Brother?"

I nodded.

"Runaways?"

I felt Sammy's forehead again, trying to tell if he was cooler, but it had only been a few minutes. "Thanks for the pill."

"I carry them in case. You'll need to wake him every half hour or so and feed him as much water as you can. The fever dehydrates you."

"Okay."

He looked at me, this time narrowing his eyes a bit. "Nothing's for free."

My heart stopped and I clutched the knife tighter.

He looked at it, then at the fire ring. Chicken bones lay around it. "You got any food?"

I opened my pack and took out the rest of the roasted chicken wrapped in my shirt, holding it for a moment. We didn't have anything else. "Here." I threw it to him.

He caught it. "That all you got?"

"Yes."

He looked at my pack. "You sure?"

"Don't call me a liar."

He chuckled, unwrapping the chicken. "Desperate times call for desperate measures."

"I'm not a liar."

"Calm down." He picked a thigh and sank his teeth in it.

I looked around the clearing. "Is there water around here?"

He nodded, his mouth full. "Back around there. A rivulet that leads to the river. You'll need purification tablets. Got any?"

"No." We'd been drinking dirty water anyway, but I figured they'd be helpful.

He dug in his pack, taking out a small brown bottle and throwing it to me. "Lifesavers. Get 'em at the army surplus." He pointed to the blankets. "Looks like you know army surplus."

I picked up the empty jar of water. "I can't leave him alone with you."

Craig picked meat from a bone. "Can't or won't?"

"Won't."

"Then you've got another decision to make. He needs water."

I stood, studying him while he ate, then pointed behind him with the knife. "Down there?"

He nodded.

Past the edge of camp I ran, and it was farther than I expected. When I found the trickle, I couldn't see the camp at all and held my breath while the jar filled. My legs screamed as I ran back up the slope, and when I reached camp, Craig was kneeling over Sammy.

I dropped the jar and bolted toward them, coming in low and fast with the knife. Just before I reached them, Craig saw me and rolled to the side. I screeched to a halt and faced him, my chest heaving as I braced him with the knife.

"Whoa!" he said, crouching with his arms up. "Lay off, man! Jesus Christ, I wasn't hurting him! He started coughing is all!"

I looked at Sammy, who sat up lethargically and rubbed his eyes. I hadn't heard a cough. "You okay, Sam?" I said, keeping my eyes on Craig.

"Who's he?"

I traded glances with the two, then lowered the knife. "I'm sorry. I thought you were hurting him."

Craig shook his head, angry. "No way, man. You almost killed me. You *would've* killed me if I hadn't seen you."

I stared at him and knew he was right. I would have killed him. "I thought you were hurting him," I repeated.

Craig stood and looked at Sammy for a moment, then walked to his pack.

"You're leaving?" I said.

He nodded, picking up his gear. "You're over the edge, kid."

"I said I was sorry." I didn't realize how much I needed somebody around. Craig didn't answer but walked from camp. As he passed the water jar I'd dropped, he stopped, picking it up.

I was about to say thanks when he raised it above his head and threw it down. The glass shattered and the water glimmered like a million lost sparkles in the morning light. His eyes met mine for a split second, then he turned and disappeared down the slope. I stared at the glass shards and darkened soil with an emptiness I couldn't control.

"Ian?" I turned, and Sammy lay looking at me. "What happened?"

I went to him, kneeling down and wiping my tears on my sleeve. "Nothing. You feel better?"

"Why are you crying, Ian?"

"I'm not." I fumbled his hand into mine and noticed it was cooler than before. "Did he touch you?"

"Who was that guy?" He was still groggy, and though the fever had gone down, he was sicker than I'd ever seen him.

"Craig. Were you awake?"

"He was saying something to me or something."

"Answer me, Sam. Are you okay?"

Sammy closed his eyes, nodding.

"What was he doing, Sam? Tell me."

"Were you going to kill him like he said?"

I squeezed my eyes shut and couldn't keep the tears away. "No, Sam, I wasn't. He just scared me is all. It's okay. You're going to get better, and everything is going to be fine. Just go back to sleep." I still had the other half of the pill and the bottle of water tablets, but no way to bring water to him.

Sammy closed his eyes and murmured something about Mom and wanting to be home and then finding our dad and having a big bed to sleep in. I stayed next to him, taking his hand back in mine and sitting with his head in my lap.

Chapter Fourteen

For the next three hours, I ran down to the creek every half hour, soaked a T-shirt with as much water as it would hold, and ran back, squeezing the water into Sammy's mouth and watching for any sign that the medicine wasn't what Craig said it was. After a while, with no convulsions or anything else alarming, I relaxed a little bit.

Without being able to dissolve the purification tablets, I worried about him getting some kind of water disease, but I couldn't do anything about it, and we'd been drinking creek water for days anyway. His fever came back, and I gave him the other half of the pill.

A half hour later, he was still burning up, and panic began clawing its way into my chest. I grabbed my pack and took the phone out, staring at it. I should call Ms. Veer or 911 or something. I flipped the lid up, turned on the power, and punched through the address book. There, under the *S* heading, was Candice Schmidt. Coach Schmidt? I'd never known her first name. I also noticed Principal Spence's name. I dialed the coach's number, and it turned out to be her phone at school. I listened to the recorded message, and at the end she gave her home number in case of emergencies. I hung up and dialed. It rang three times.

"Hello?"

"Coach?"

"Yes. Who am I speaking to?"

"Ian McDermott."

She paused. "Ian?"

"Yeah."

"Where are you?"

"I need help."

Silence.

"My brother is sick."

"Where are you?"

"Away. I need your help."

"You should really call . . . ," she began, then stopped. "Tell me."

"He's got a fever. I gave him a pill, but it came back and it's not going away."

"What kind of pill?"

"I don't know, but the first half of it made the fever go down. Now it's not working."

"Where are you, Ian? You've got to get him to a doctor."

"In the forest. How do you make a fever go away?"

"Take his clothes off. Do you have water?"

"Sort of." I struggled with his pants.

"Wet a shirt or something if you have it and swab his body with it. Try and keep things cool for him, okay?" she said. "Listen, Ian, you've got to get him help."

"I'm talking to you, aren't I?"

"I know, but you—"

123

"We don't have anywhere to go, okay? Just hang up if you don't want to help me."

Silence again. "Okay, get his clothes off and wipe him down with the T-shirt. And if you can, get him to drink as much as you can."

"That'll help?"

"It should."

"Okay. I've got to go."

"No, Ian, don't. Tell me where you are."

"So you can call the cops? No thanks."

"Ian, please, your brother—"

I flipped the phone closed, half mad and half guilty for dissing her after she'd helped me, then took the rest of Sammy's clothes off, using the wet T-shirt to pat him down like she'd instructed. I sat with him until his forehead wasn't burning, and by midafternoon my panic ebbed with his fever. I knew that if he felt better by the night, he'd have to eat. The chicken in my stomach was long gone, and I had the shakes big-time. If I didn't get something myself, I'd end up lying next to him, suffering, too.

I'd heard voices off in the distance several hours earlier, so I got up and started walking in that direction, the sound of cars whizzing by on the highway reaching me before I came to the main area of the park. At the end of the parking area and near the restrooms, I saw signs pointing toward a camping area, then my eye caught two garbage cans at each entrance to the restrooms.

The parking lot was deserted, so I went to the first can and started scrounging through it. After digging through the wrappers and avoiding the sticky or wet things, I came up with two empty Gatorade bottles, complete with lids. My lucky day. I washed them out in the bathroom sink and filled them, drank one down, refilled it, then stuffed my pockets with as much toilet paper as I could before returning outside and sitting on a bench. *No more leaves,* I thought, and my butt was already thanking me.

I looked at the plastic bottles with the clear water in them and smiled. Two quarts of water would go a long way, and half of my problem was solved. A few minutes later, a blue Ford Taurus pulled into the lot and parked in front of the restrooms. A pudgy guy in a dress shirt and tie, loosened at the neck, sat in the driver's seat. He shut the engine off and threw his cigarette, half smoked, out the window.

From the expression on his face, he was pinching something back in a big way, and he barely looked at me as he beelined for the crapper. I eyed the car for a minute. Everything screamed traveling salesman. The car was fifty yards away. I sprinted to it, keeping my eye on the bathroom door as I did so.

I poked my head in the driver-side window and there, on the passenger seat, was a lunch cooler. Next to it was a copy of *Penthouse* magazine. Prying my eyes from the boob-filled cover, I lurched through the window and grabbed the cooler, yanking it out and running back to the bench. With the cooler in one hand and the bottles cradled against me, I ran.

A few minutes later, I was back in camp, breathless and shaking, but with my treasures intact and no furious guy running after me. Sammy lay still, his breathing even, and I touched his forehead. A bit warm, but still okay.

I sat next to him and stared at the cooler. At this point, the thought of stealing some guy's cooler didn't really bug me, and I didn't stop then to think about how desperation makes it easier to break the rules. We needed food, and I got it. End of story. I knew there was stuff in it because of its weight, and felt like a little kid when I put my hands on the lid. This was my treasure box and the surprise was inside.

I waited a second or two longer, looking at the blue and white thing like it might hold a million dollars, then opened it. Amid the ice and water I found three-quarters of a hoagie, the wrapper of another eaten one, a single serving of strawberry-flavored applesauce, a Pepsi, and three cans of beer. Down at the bottom and under the ice I found three plastic-wrapped sticks of pepperoni, too. Enough to get us by, and I had a few beers in case friends dropped by. Not bad.

I couldn't bring myself to eat the sandwich. I stared at it, and my stomach screamed at me to at least take half, but with Sammy the way he was, I just couldn't do it. I did eat two pepperoni sticks and slurped down half the applesauce, and ten minutes later, my hands stopped shaking.

Sammy slept as the sun fell past the trees, and I set about gathering wood for a fire. This far south, the nights weren't as cold, but I still wanted it. Half an hour later, Sammy stirred and sat up. In the dusk and with the fire casting the beginnings of long shadows around us, he looked pale. Deathly pale. But he wasn't whining or crying, and for that I was glad. It meant he was getting better. He sat Indian-style, staring at the fire and sipping water from his Gatorade bottle, finally pulling a blanket over him as the night cooled.

We didn't talk for a long while, he and I next to each other, and I drank two beers as twilight set in and the stars came out. I think it had finally sunk in for him that we weren't going home, and I was a bit sad that it had to be that way.

I felt the buzz from the beers, and my chest loosened, tension melting away that I hadn't even known was there before. Sam told me he was hungry, and I unwrapped the sandwich for him. He ate slowly, like an old man, and it took fifteen minutes for him to get it down. His fever was gone but his eyes were still glazed, and I hoped the worst was over.

We sat for hours in front of that fire, not saying a word as we stared into the flames, and I wondered where our lives were going. I don't know if it was the beers or the silence, but I knew right then that I never wanted to go back. It didn't matter what happened tomorrow or the next day or what we'd find at the address in Walla Walla or if our father was even alive. I never wanted to see our house—or that life—again.

I didn't want to wake up every morning wondering where Mom was or what we'd have to eat or what would happen next. The dealers and dope and lies and garbage were gone. I missed Blind Man Thompson from across the street, and Bennie was the truest, best friend I'd ever had, but those flames told me that going back to them meant going back to everything else, and I couldn't do that. The only thing that mattered was Sammy. And me.

I wondered again why our father left and wondered, too, if he'd made the same choice I did. I could see him waking up one morning and realizing that the rest of his life wasn't worth it. That there might be something else out there, and what he had just wasn't good enough. I drank the last half of the third beer, wondering if his decision left room for us coming back into his life, then decided it wasn't worth thinking about.

Sammy drank the rest of his water and curled up next to me, and in a few minutes, his breathing evened out. I glanced at my pack a couple of times, then reached over and set it on my lap, taking the phone out.

I began dialing Bennie's number and found I couldn't focus

too easily on the keypad. Halfway through I stopped, then dialed Veronica Jorgenson's number instead. I didn't have to jump through hoops with her dad because she had a phone in her room, and she picked up after three rings. "Veronica?"

"Ian? Oh my God. Are you in jail?"

"No."

"Where are you?"

I didn't answer, but leaned back and stared at the stars.

"Ian?"

"Yeah?"

"Are you okay?"

"Sammy's sick."

"Sick like real sick? What's going on? Where are you? The cops are still after you, you know. Coach Florence has his jaw wired. You broke it."

The last thing in the world I wanted to think about was him. "I figured."

Veronica went on. "Bennie needs to talk to you. Something about a list. He asked me to tell you if you called." She sounded puzzled at his request. "How did he know you'd call me?"

I pictured her face in the stars, connecting the dots as I thought about her. "I don't know. He's weird that way."

"Well." She giggled. "He was right. How sick is your brother?"

"Sammy's getting better now. That's not why I called."

"Why did you call, then?"

"Why did you break up with me?" I heard her breathe over the line and knew she was thinking. I couldn't get Principal Spence's words out of my head. They haunted me. *For a person with your aptitude* . . .

"I don't know. Things just happen."

"Tell me."

"I don't know, Ian. I like you. I do. It's just that I couldn't see things working, you know?"

"Your dad?"

"Maybe. He doesn't like guys like you."

"And that's why you do?"

"You know it's not that way."

"Bennie told me you were slumming."

"That's not true, Ian. I wasn't slumming."

"Then what is true, Veronica?"

"It just wouldn't have worked out."

"Why?"

"I don't know. It just wouldn't."

"Because of what I am?"

She wouldn't answer.

"Expectations, right?" I threw a twig into the fire, the alcohol still swimming through my veins.

"What?"

"Expectations. We can't have you shacking up with a guy like me, you know? Daddy's girl needs more than a two-bedroom down on Fifth with a guy working sixty hours a week at minimum to pay the bills, right?"

"Ian . . ."

"Don't bother. I know what the shit is and what the shit isn't, Veronica. Bye." I flipped the phone shut and stared at it, tempted to throw it in the fire. I dialed Coach Schmidt's number instead. "Hi."

"Ian?"

"Yep."

"Is your brother doing better?"

I looked at him. "His name is Sammy. Yes. He's sleeping."

"Good."

"Thanks."

An awkward silence followed, then she cleared her throat. "You know, I should tell you to turn yourself in, Ian. This isn't a good situation."

I laughed. "Really? I hadn't noticed."

"What are you going to do now?"

"Life on the run, babe." I smiled at the flames, the beer still running through me.

"Babe?"

"Sorry. You probably don't like guys saying that to you."

Her voice lowered. "Ian . . . ," she started, then paused. "That is none of your business."

"Just like Bennie's dad isn't Jeff Stearns's business, right? We're all supposed to ignore the bad stuff, huh?" I sighed, staring into the fire. "Just let it *slide*."

The line crackled, and she didn't say anything. She'd no doubt heard about our fight. "That was about Ben?"

I laughed. "I took care of it. No worries, huh? Don't have to go expelling one of Morrison High's treasures."

She put two and two together, remembering the wrestler's stay in the hospital. "You have a penchant for brutal justice, don't you?"

"Don't tell me you haven't wanted to take Coach Florence out. Or Spence. And don't tell me you couldn't, either. They hate you."

This time she laughed. "I won't say the thought hasn't crossed my mind."

"Can I ask you a question, Coach?"

"Shoot."

"Why didn't you stop me?"

"When you hit Coach Florence?"

"Yeah. You could have. You could have held me until school security got there."

She hesitated. "I couldn't chance another confrontation on school grounds. It was better you go."

"Bullshit."

She breathed into the phone. "Well, my reasons are my own, then."

"Fair enough."

"Ian, I don't want to see you go through this. Living on the street is no way to live. Whose phone are you on?"

"Ms. Veer's."

Silence.

"She gave it to me. Don't worry, I didn't steal it. Just food and beer." I laughed.

"You've been drinking?"

"Yeah. But I won't drive. I was thinking about hopping on down to McDonald's, then catching a movie, but I'm sort of tired."

"I'm serious, Ian."

"Me too. Sammy's fine now, and I had a few beers. They were in a cooler I stole today. We needed to eat, and the brews were an added bonus."

"Ian . . ."

"Have you ever picked food out of a garbage can for dinner, Coach?"

"No."

"Then don't talk to me about stealing. Or drinking a few beers."

"What are you going to do now?"

"Keep going."

"We can get this straightened out if you come back."

"We? *We* is you, and you turn us over to them, and they don't give a shit about me or Sammy, so what's the point?"

"They? Who are they, Ian? You think the whole world is out to get you?"

"They. You know who they are, Coach, because they don't like you, either."

That stopped her.

I went on. "Tell me they like you, Coach. Go ahead. Say they wouldn't give all the money in the world to get you out. Spence, Florence, all those assholes in the district. You know they tell jokes about you and talk behind your back and all that good stuff. You're the embarrassment of the district."

"That doesn't matter, and this isn't about me. It's about you."

I laughed. "So there *is* a they. See, Coach, the 'they' for me is all those people, plus cops and judges and social workers and foster homes and truancy officers and God. The world doesn't like people like us, and I never thought I'd say it, but Bennie is right. It's the *system,* and it's set up for people like me. 'Cept I don't want it. I can ruin my life on my own just fine."

"Sounds like you're ready to quit."

"Quit?"

"Yes, Ian. Quit. Those are the words of a quitter."

"I'm not quitting anything."

"You ran away. Weak people run."

I laughed. "No, no, no. I see where this is going. I'm not coming back to face your system, Coach. I'm done doing push-ups while *players* stand and watch, and taking shit from guys like

Florence and listening to the principal of my school tell me he wants me gone because he's *cleaning up this school* and that Kerner would be good for a guy with *my aptitude.*" I laughed again, shaking my head. "And that's just the start. I come back and I deal with the courts and cops, and Sammy is a goner. You know what happens when you have a drug addict for a mother, Coach? You know what it feels like to have somebody look at you and see just another future inmate or loser or druggie or scumbag? Makes me feel all warm inside."

She zeroed in on Spence. "Spence told you that?"

"What the hell did you think would happen after you talked to him? You think Vice Principal Veer knows what the hell she's doing? She's an idiot. Spence got wind of it, and that was it. End of story. In fact, he can *guarantee* that if I stay at Morrison, it won't be good." I sneered, half laughing because now, in the middle of nowhere with a sick brother and a gnawing in my gut that said as much about hopelessness as hunger, it was a joke. The whole thing was a joke. "How the heck do you think Kerner Alternative gets students? The volunteer system? You don't fit, you think Morrison High makes room for you? Jesus, Coach, you should know how it works by now."

Coach Schmidt sighed. "Listen, Ian, I don't think I should be talking to you like this. I think you should come back and face your life. Even if it is the way you say, nobody can change it but you. I think maybe if you begin taking responsibility for your actions, you'll see it's not the world against you, but you against yourself."

"Thanks for the sermon, Coach." I flipped the phone shut and stared in the fire. I thought about what she said. How was I against myself? Then I thought of Craig and him breaking the water jar after I nearly killed him. Maybe Coach Schmidt was right. Craig had been trying to help, and I'd screwed it up because I assumed he was out to hurt us.

I added a couple sticks to the fire and stared at the phone in my hand. I opened it and dialed. "Ms. Veer?"

"Ian?"

"How'd you know it was me?"

"I have caller ID. It showed my cell number. Are you all right?"

"No."

"What can I do?"

"How is Coach Florence?"

"His jaw is broken, but he's doing well. Where are you?"

"I'm not coming back."

Her tone was soft. "I've made some calls."

"About what?"

She hesitated. "You told me that my kind of help didn't work, Ian, and I understand how you could feel that way. I realized that maybe you're right. Maybe I was looking at this from only one perspective. . . ."

"Your perspective."

She cleared her throat. "Yes. My perspective. But that has changed."

I leaned back, glancing at Sammy to make sure he was breathing easy. "You made calls?"

"Yes. I did. I've been in contact with a man named Phinias Magnuson. He's a friend of mine."

"Who is he?"

"He works with the juvenile courts as a counselor for teens. An intermediary who looks out for kids as they go through the system."

I roll my eyes. "Great."

"No, listen, Ian. Please. This is the only thing I can do within the law, and I don't have to. This isn't a part of my job, Ian. I want to do this. I've explained to him the circumstances of what happened and I've told him about you. Good things. He's interested in helping you and Sammy, and I trust him."

"We're not coming back."

"I understand that. But if you do, I'll be here and Phinias can help. He's good, Ian, and I think you'd like him. He has a lot of experience in dealing with the courts, and he sees things a different way. I'm just asking you to think about it, okay?"

I stared at the stars, wondering if she was right. Maybe he could get Sammy help. The right kind of help.

"At least think about it?"

"Sure."

"Are you safe?"

"I've got to go."

"You can do this, Ian. I know you can. Come home."

I wasn't sure if she was right, and I didn't think the beer helped things, either. "Thanks, Ms. Veer."

Then I hung up.

Chapter Fifteen

I woke up with Sammy staring at me. "I'm better."

I rubbed the sleep from my eyes. I don't know how late it'd been when I finally fell asleep, but I knew only a few hours had passed. I'd meant to call Bennie and ask him about this "list" Veronica had been talking about, but I'd fallen asleep. "Hungry?"

Sammy nodded.

After last night on the phone and the beers and everything we'd gone through to get exactly nowhere, any pride I had was gone. I thought about Ms. Veer and her kind of help, but I couldn't turn back. Something in me couldn't trust her. Sammy was too important. We had to continue.

We packed up what little we had and went down to the river, washing up as best we could and laying in the sun for a few minutes to dry off. The only thing to think about was reaching the address in Walla Walla. There was nothing else.

Central Ferry State Park looked to be around thirty or forty miles from Walla Walla, and as I looked across the river, I noticed the country was much harsher, with rocky scrub desert, sheer drop-offs, and deep ravines. My heart sank with the thought of even trying to go cross-country.

We trudged up the embankment and made our way through the park, coming to the highway where a bridge ran across the river and keeping a lookout for cops. "Well, Sam, you can say you've been to the Snake River," I said, marveling at how big it was from up above on the bridge.

"Why'd they call it that? Are there snakes in it?"

I shook my head. "I think because it winds a lot, like a snake."

He gazed at the ribbon of water. "Cool."

"I think we're going to get to Walla Walla today."

He brightened. "Really? You said we had a bunch more miles to go."

"We're going to get a lift. Just keep your eyes out for cops coming from that way"—I pointed across the bridge, then turned back and stuck my thumb out—"and I'll look this way."

We stood by the side of the road for fifteen minutes and I couldn't believe how many pickup trucks, touring motorcycles, and big rigs passed us. Every once in a while, a family in a minivan or a solitary guy in a sedan would zip by, but for the most part, it was farmers and truckers and touring bikers on their Gold Wings.

Standing at the bridge, the sun beat down, leaving us wet with sweat. Sammy sat and kept an eye out for cops, and I stood there, shifting my feet every once in a while with my thumb stuck out, nervous that we'd be caught. Then a guy in a new pickup truck with silver toolboxes lining the bed pulled over and motioned for us to get in.

We scrambled to the passenger-side door, and the driver, a middle-aged guy in a baseball cap and T-shirt, scooted several files into a briefcase and threw it on the floorboards. "Hop in, boys."

We did. He put it in gear and we were off. His name was Jacob Mallory, and he lived in Endicott. He was an engineer for a road construction company, and he was working a job on the outskirts of Walla Walla, and he liked to talk. He had three boys and a wife who stayed home with them while he was working, and he was soft-spoken when he asked what we were doing in the middle of nowhere. Sammy told him we were going to see our father, and Jacob didn't reply, several miles passing before he spoke again. "Your father, huh?"

I nodded, glancing out the window and watching the hell-like terrain we weren't having to walk across. "Yeah. He lives in Walla Walla."

He glanced at his watch. "I probably have time to drop you at his place if it's this side of town."

"How much further?" Sammy said. He was holding his fingers in front of the air-conditioning vent.

"Thirty miles."

"Long way when you're walking," Sammy said, and I nudged him.

Jacob smiled. "I take it you've come a long way?"

"Spokane," I said.

"You walked?" He raised his eyebrows, laughing.

"Yeah."

He stopped laughing. "No shit?"

"Well, almost the whole way."

He adjusted his cap. "Must be some kind of dad, then."

Sammy put his fingers on his cheek, feeling the cold. "We've never met him."

This time I jabbed him in the ribs, and he shut up.

"Oh," Jacob said. "Get in a bit of trouble up Spokane way?"

"Just going to see our dad," I said.

He slowed for a curve. "None of my business anyway." A few minutes of silence followed, with me staring at the painted lines running by and him setting the cruise control on the truck. "You boys came down past Endicott?"

I nodded, eyeing his lunch cooler next to the briefcase.

"Few days ago we had a sheriff up 'round there, little north it was, get into a bit of trouble. Couple of kids in that storm we had. Busted up his knee. Caused quite a ruckus with people."

The only thing I could hear was my heart hammering my rib cage. We hadn't come this far to get busted thirty miles outside of town. "You can let us out now."

He smiled. "Don't be so quick about things, now. I ain't saying something one way or another. Just making conversation."

I took a breath. He knew, and there was nothing I could do about it, because I'd had enough. Of everything. Sammy and I fit the description perfectly, and Jacob knew as well as I did that the chances of two pairs of runaways wandering around were just about zero. I thought more about it, and until now, I didn't realize how much leaving the sheriff stranded had bothered me. There was no use in lying. Jacob knew. "Is he all right?"

"John Walker and I went to high school together." He glanced our way. "That's his name."

My heart sank. Just our luck that this guy would know him. "Is he okay?"

"He'll be fine. I hear some surgery might be in order, but the bones weren't busted."

Sammy piped up. "I was the one who hit him, not Ian. So you could just let him go and take me."

"You know," he said, "I wasn't born an engineer. Fact is, I've had my own scrapes with the law, and I'll tell you one thing, sometimes you've got to do bad things to get to the good things." He drove for a few seconds. "John Walker is a good man."

He let that hang, and I had a feeling he was waiting for something. "We can't go back," I said.

He glanced at us. "You don't strike me as the kind to wander around hurting people for no reason, even if you are looking a bit desperate."

"We're not."

"Runaways, I figured."

I nodded. "You're not going to turn us in?"

"You said you're going to find your dad?"

"Yes."

"Then what?"

I thought about that. "I guess try and make things better."

He took a moment. "Tell you what. I'll drop you where you need if you give me your word you'll set things right with John Walker after the situation settles down."

I grunted, staring out the window. "I'm sure the judge will do that."

He shook his head. "Not talking about the judge. I'm talking about making something wrong right. You do that, and I'll take you."

I pictured the sheriff in a hospital bed with his knee all bandaged up. "I will."

Jacob drove, and I told him the address. 1313 North Thirteenth Street. He glanced at us sideways, opened his mouth, then shut it. "You superstitious?"

"No."

A shadow crossed his face. "I know that address. Take you right there."

"Thanks."

He pointed to the cooler. "Go ahead."

"We're fine. Thanks."

"You keep eyeing that thing like it'll open itself up and feed you. Go ahead."

Sammy and I ate ham sandwiches, one each, and shared chips and a cookie while Jacob drove. Jacob's wife fixed him lunch every morning, and she was a great sandwich fixer. Just enough mustard and cheese and lettuce. He told us he'd been arrested several times when he was a teenager. The last time, when he was eighteen, had been for armed robbery. He'd robbed a convenience store so he could pay the mortgage on his mom's house, and he spent three years in prison for it. I guessed that's what he meant by doing bad things for good reasons.

We drove into Walla Walla, and Jacob told us that there were a large number of Hispanics living in the area. Agriculture, he said, and they work damn hard to make a living. The freeway was nearly empty as we took a City Center exit, and I counted the streets from First Street to Thirteenth before he took a right at a tractor business. A mile or so down the road, he took a left into a gated parking lot. The engine idled. "Well, here you go."

I looked around. The parking lot was enormous, and I watched people walking to and from their cars, coming and going up a set of stairs to a small white building. Sprinklers misted hundreds of yards of grass leading up a slope to a complex of brick and concrete buildings. "This is it?" I said.

"You didn't know, did you?" Jacob said.

Then I saw it. Burned into the grass slope in ten-foot-high letters was PENITENTIARY. I stared at it.

"I'm sorry," Jacob said. "This is where I spent my time."

My heart slid into my stomach. I nudged Sammy. "Open the door, Sam."

Jacob waved as he pulled out of the parking lot, leaving us facing the prison alone. Past the white building sat a tall brick structure, and behind that, concrete walls with huge turrets—guard stations, I guessed—were interspersed along the perimeter. Our father was in prison.

"What is this?" Sam said.

I pointed. "The Washington State Penitentiary."

"What's a penitentiary?"

"It means our dad is in prison."

"He's in jail?"

"Prison. Jail but worse." We stood in the parking lot next to a beat-up Astro van. All this for nothing. No house, no job, no good life. Prison. Nothing different in our lives, and I was an idiot for dreaming of anything else.

I saw my future beyond that white building, and it tugged at me. It pissed me off. It was everything everybody expected of me, and this was like the ultimate joke. I realized then that hope, for whatever reason, didn't work in real life. My life was set in stone, just like those gun turrets jabbing the sky, and there wasn't a thing I could do to get away from it. We had nowhere to go.

I took the phone from my pack and dialed Bennie's cell number. He answered on the third ring. "Hi, Ben." I stared at the prison as I talked.

"Whoa. In class here, buddy. Call me back in three minutes."

I did, and it rang twice before he answered. "Where are you now, Ben?"

"Bathroom. I just got detention for answering in class. Where the hell are you? I've got news."

"The penitentiary."

"Damn. You didn't kill the guy. Just broke his jaw."

I stared at the turrets. "Not that. Our dad is here."

Silence. "I'm sorry, man."

"Don't be."

"Did you meet him?"

"Tell me a good reason and I will."

"Pity party for Ian. Everybody go boo-hoo."

I felt the tears build but held them back. "Sorry, man. It's just fucked up. Everything is. The address could have been anywhere, Ben, but it just *has* to be here. Nowhere but here. It's like everything in my whole life leads straight down a road I don't want to go."

"You should go see him. At least look at him or something. Tell him he's a jerk and walk out. My counselor told me in a moment of lucid thought that I should address issues head-on."

"No."

"Your choice, then, but I think you're wrong."

"Veronica told me about some list you have."

"*I* don't have it, but somebody does. Somebody you know."

"What is it, Ben? Don't play the mystery game here."

"Okay, here's the story. . . ." He paused, gathering his thoughts. I heard a lighter flick and the sound of him inhaling. Then he exhaled. "So, after you clock Florence, everybody and their mother is talking about it, right? Typical bullshit. Then I hear Holden Fenway talking with his buddies in the cafeteria. You know Holden, right?"

I did. Holden was the best pitcher Morrison High had recruited in twenty years. They'd gotten him from a small farm school fifteen miles out of town. He had the majors stamped all over him. "Yeah, I know him."

"Well, he's talking about this list that Principal Spence has. A list of students."

It all clicked. "And I was on it."

"That's what Holden said when I got in his face, anyway."

I shrugged. I'd known Spence wanted me gone for a while, and a stupid list didn't change any of that. "Spence told me he was cleaning up the school, Bennie. So he has a list. Big deal."

"There's more, Ian, and I've been thinking about it. It's not just the troublemakers. Hell, I'm worse than you, and I haven't heard a peep from Spence. It's something else."

"What, then?"

"Shit, gotta go."

A deeper voice echoed over the phone, then the line went dead. I assumed Bennie had just been busted for smoking in the bathroom. The battery meter was down to one bar, so I turned the phone off and stuffed it in my pack. What kind of list? What could it mean? I knew that rumors flew around the school like mini tornadoes, and that half of them weren't true, but something was happening, and Bennie wouldn't say anything unless he was sure. Or as sure as Bennie could be. But none of it mattered anyway because we weren't going back. "Let's go, Sam." I turned my back on the prison and began walking toward the gate that Jacob had driven from.

"Ian . . ." Sammy stood alone, not budging from his spot.

I turned. "Sammy, there's no use, okay? He can't help us. He can't do anything. Not from there."

"You said we'd see him, and I want to. His name is Samuel."

I raised my voice. "He's in prison, Sam! Jesus, don't be this way. Don't you see? There's nothing here for us! Or anywhere!" He kept staring at me. "What? You want to see him? Ask him

144

what he did to get here? Is that going to make you feel good? He's a loser, Sam, so forget it."

"I want to see him, and you promised."

I looked from him to the prison. It struck me that something so nice-looking, with the sprinklers and grass and flower beds and brick, could also be something terrible. Sammy didn't cry or yell or whine, and I think it was because, just like me, he was done in. There was nowhere else to go. "Fine. We'll go in."

Chapter Sixteen

We trudged up the stairs and entered the white building. Two guards stood looking out the windows and one guard, balding and pudgy, sat behind a Plexiglas partition, eyeing us with dull expectancy. I left Sam shuffling his feet by the door and stepped to the Plexiglas. There was a hole cut in it to speak through. When I didn't say anything, he did. "Can I help you?"

I looked out the window to the right, glancing at the turrets and the guards walking around. "We're here to see Samuel McDermott."

"Names?" he said, glancing down at a list on the counter.

"Sam and Ian McDermott."

He clicked a pen down the list, shaking his head. "You're not on the list. No McDermott."

"You have to be on a list?"

He nodded, then turned to a computer, furrowing his brow. "Gimme a sec here. My first full day working here, and this computer . . ." He turned his attention to the monitor. "No. I'm not showing a Samuel McDermott incarcerated here anyway. Sure you have the right name?"

"He's not here anymore?"

He reached under the counter and began pulling another notebook out when one of the other guards, who had been staring at Sammy, stepped up. "Did you say Samuel McDermott?"

I nodded.

The second guard gestured to the wall. "Please step over there with your partner." He grabbed another notebook, flipped through it, then picked up the phone. I took my place next to Sam and heard the guard talking in low tones into the receiver. After a moment, he hung up and spoke to the other guard. Then he walked over to us. "Hang tight for a few, huh? I will need to search your packs before I take you in." After raising his eyebrows at the knife in my pack and passing it through the Plexiglas window, he handed our gear back and told us to follow him. We did.

Through the white building, we ended up on a walkway with grass on either side, heading toward the brick building. Once inside, we followed the guard to the foyer, where a dark-haired lady in a business jacket and skirt met us. She introduced herself as Jannette Mills, then led us through two locked doors, where guards buzzed us through to an elevator.

The doors opened three floors up, where she exited, telling us to follow. Down a short hall and to the right, we came to a wooden door with a plaque on it reading SUPERINTENDENT. Inside was an empty desk—Jannette's, I figured—and a waiting area of sorts. Beyond that and to the right was another door. She asked us to sit and then took a seat behind her desk, pushing a button on the phone.

We sat. I studied her, my heart beating a bit faster than usual. "Did we do something wrong?"

She looked up and smiled. "The superintendent will be with you in a moment."

Sammy kicked his feet under the chair, swinging them back and forth until I touched his knee to make him stop. We sat in leather chairs, and there was a table in front of us with magazines lined up neatly. A few plants hung in the corners, and a picture of a sailboat caught in a storm, its mast snapped in two as waves crashed over its bow, hung on one wall. Somehow it was fitting.

A few minutes later, the phone buzzed and Jannette stood. "This way, please."

I knew this wasn't the usual protocol for people visiting inmates, and while one part of me wondered what was going on, another part didn't care. My existence could be spent sitting in the warden's office just as easily as by the side of the road, hitching a ride to who knows where. Sammy and I stood while Jannette opened the door and ushered us in, shutting it as we stepped inside the office.

A man stood at the corner of a huge oak desk. At least six-five, he wore a tie and dress slacks. For a moment, I thought I was looking at a huge version of Sammy. I realized I was standing in front of my father.

Samuel McDermott stood there, studying us with the same eyes we studied him with. The same dark hair, the same ears, the same nose. Our father was the warden of the Washington State Penitentiary. An awkward minute of silence followed, then he took his hand out of his pocket. "Ian and Samuel McDermott."

"You're our dad?" Sammy said, unsure of himself.

He nodded. "I am. Samuel McDermott."

"We thought . . . ," Sammy started.

He nodded again. "I know. One of the guards overheard your name and happened to see the resemblance." He smiled. "It is unmistakable."

Sammy looked around the office, and I kept my eyes on the big figure standing in front of us. I had his eyes and more of his build than Sammy, but Sammy's face was dead-on the same—the cheekbones, jaw, lips, and hair. But our father looked more clean-cut in his suit and cufflinks and nice hair. We were dirty and scroungy, and I realized with a sense of desperation that the last place I wanted to be right now was here. Not like this, anyway. "We got here and thought you were an inmate." I repeated the thought, not knowing what else to say.

His eyes softened. "I take it your mother hasn't talked about me much."

I shook my head.

He gestured to the seats in front of his desk. "Sit down." We did, and he took a seat, too. "How did you get here?"

I didn't want to start things off by lying, but I didn't really want to tell him. "We walked most of the way."

He raised his eyebrows. "You're hungry?"

Sammy piped up. "Starving."

I cut in. "We ate already."

Samuel picked up the phone. "Jannette, have two lunches brought up immediately." He looked me up and down. "Extra portions." Then he hung up.

I looked at his desk, and there, next to a penholder, was a picture of a woman standing with two children, each younger than Sammy and me. A boy and a girl. The boy looked like Sammy. The girl looked like the woman. I tried to imagine me in that picture, wearing a faded black Ramones T-shirt with my hair spiked up and my piercings glinting in the camera's eye, and I wilted. I could never fit in that picture with him. Sammy couldn't, either.

He saw me looking, and an expression, almost guilty, came to

149

his face. Like he wished he'd taken the picture away before we got there. He gazed out the window, then swung his eyes back to me. "I've thought about this day."

I stared into his eyes and knew why he left us. Compared to the picture, who wouldn't? "Is it like you thought?"

He shook his head. "I don't think that really matters, Ian. What matters is that you're here."

"We ran away," Sammy said.

He nodded. "How is your mother?"

"Ask her," I said.

He nodded again. "I guess I deserve that."

I couldn't keep it down any longer. The house. The CD player in my own room. The fenced yard with a dog. I looked at the picture of his family and wondered for a millisecond if we would get along, then I looked at Sammy sitting there in his filth and it didn't matter. Our father had all those things, but they weren't for us. I could see it in his eyes. But he'd said, "How is your mother?" like he did care, and it made me mad for some reason.

"Last time we saw her, she was whoring herself out to pay for drugs. Is that what you thought, too? You know, when you were wondering about this day?"

He winced. "Ian . . ."

I shook my head. "This was a mistake."

"No. It wasn't."

"Why?"

He sighed. "I'm not immune to making mistakes in my life, boys. . . ."

Here it goes, I thought. The excuses start now. "Mistakes? Ever hear of child support?" I glared at him. "Maybe visits every once in a while? Or what, were you waiting until we were old enough to come live with you here?" I gestured to the prison around us. "That's where people like us end up, right? That's why you left, right?" I pointed to the picture. "You got it all, huh?"

He clenched his teeth, frustrated, then reached into a drawer. He took out a file and slid it across the desk to me. The tab read *Ian and Samuel*. I opened it up. The title on the first page read *Peterson Rentals*. The second page was titled *Ridgeview Apartments*. Several more with different titles followed. All places we'd lived. We'd lived at the Ridgeview Apartments before moving into the house. I saw numbers below the titles. "You paid our rent?"

"Ever since I left. Your mother isn't the best money manager, so instead of sending her a check, I paid any rents due. And any medical bills due, though the state took care of most. Look in the back of the folder."

I did, taking out spreadsheets. "What?"

"Trust funds. For you and Sammy. I put equal amounts in theirs, too." He pointed to the two kids in the picture. He clasped his hands together on the desk. "I'm not a monster, Ian. I've made mistakes, and I'm sorry things have ended up like this, but I have looked out for you in my own way."

I didn't buy it. "How did you figure things would end up? How *could* you think things would end up different?" I stared at him. "She was addicted when you left, huh?"

He didn't answer.

"She was, wasn't she?"

"Yes. I was a supervisor at the corrections facility in Spokane, Ian. That's how we met. She'd cleaned herself up and was serving the last of a possession sentence, and I fell for her. She stayed clean for seven years, too."

"Seven?" I looked at Sammy. So did he.

"Yes," he said slowly.

She'd been an addict throughout her pregnancy with Sam. I

151

saw the pain in his eyes when he said it, and for some reason, the anger left me. "You tried, didn't you?"

He nodded. "Probably just like you, son."

When he said it, tears instantly came to my eyes. *Son.* My lip trembled, and I didn't like it one bit. "Don't call me that." I pointed at the picture of his family. "They're what you wanted, aren't they?"

It hurt him to say it, but he did. "Yes, they are."

"Bet you don't make many mistakes with them, do you?"

He nodded. "Yes, I do. Everybody does."

I looked at Sammy, who thankfully didn't understand half of what was being said. I stood. "We'd better go."

"No," he said, and I knew right then that he was the warden for a reason. His tone was sharp, low, and full of authority. He tried to cover it up. "No," he repeated, softer this time.

"Why?"

"Because you are in trouble, and I want to help you. I want to hear about it." He leaned back. "At least stay and eat. Let me get you set up and feeling better, and we can figure some things out."

Right then, Jannette buzzed and the door opened. She held two trays of food. Samuel gave me a pleading look. "Please?"

I nodded.

He excused himself, then, leaving us to the food, which consisted of a bowl of Mexican bean soup, two burritos each, corn, and tater tots. I didn't realize how hungry I was until I started eating, and in just a few minutes, my tray and bowl were clean.

Sam didn't say much as we sat there, drinking the last of our milk and staring at Samuel McDermott's desk. I studied the picture. They looked like nice kids. The kind you'd see at the grocery store with their mother. My head swam with thoughts about what would happen next, and I couldn't keep myself from hoping. Maybe they had an extra bedroom for us. Maybe I'd been too harsh. I was old enough to babysit, and I'd be sixteen in two months, which meant I could drive them around. I could mow the lawn, do chores and help out. I could get a job. Sammy could play with the boy who looked like him, and he could pretty much take care of himself anyway.

I figured the warden could pull strings. He was a powerful man, with this being the biggest prison in the state. He'd know people. Judges and cops and politicians would smile when they heard his name, and he could make calls. He could make this go away, and Sammy and I could start new. Fresh. I could be a straight arrow and follow the rules and get good grades and go to college. I could even dress like the kids in the picture. And Sammy could get help. Real help. The kind you pay for and not the kind the state supplied. We could, I thought, do it all if we were in that picture, too.

But as I sat there looking at his normal family and imagining everything I'd wanted so badly, it made me feel small. This wasn't for us, and I'd seen enough of that in his eyes to know I was a fool for thinking it. I didn't need to prove myself to anybody. He'd skated from our lives and not given a damn since, trust money or rent notwithstanding, and for that I hated him. He didn't deserve my respect. He didn't want our lives and he didn't want us, and for that, he could go straight to hell.

Every night we'd slept in the shed was a night he wasn't there. Every time I got hassled in school, he didn't care. All the crappy things in our lives sprang into my mind, and I hated him and hated me even more for it. He was a good father and husband and provider, just not with us, and I almost wished he *was* an inmate because then there'd be a reason for him leaving. Scumbags do what he did. They leave their children. He wasn't a scumbag, though.

And the truth was, I wanted to be in that picture more than anything else in the world. I wanted Sammy to smile when Dad came to the school for lunch and went to his baseball games and showed him how to build model airplanes and fix his bike. I wanted him to come home from work and ask me how my day went and take me to the doctor in his car instead of me humping it to some clinic by myself and sitting for hours. I wanted dinner at a table and laughing and talk and green grass with no dandelions or old ladies hassling me because of what we were. I wanted barbecues and trips to the park and all the stupid, silly things that didn't come in a box of Tuna Helper.

He might do it, and I cursed myself for flip-flopping about it. My mind raced. He might come back in and take us home. To our new home. He might make calls and smooth things over and make things all right. I did see caring in his eyes, and sadness and guilt. He could be the guy to change our lives, and I decided right then that I couldn't let my pride ruin it. Not for me or for Sammy. There was nothing else, I knew. Nowhere else to go. I had three bucks to my name, a full stomach, a skateboard, a pack full of filthy clothes, and no future. Coach Schmidt was right. We couldn't go on like this.

Sammy finished by licking the bowl of soup clean, then swung his legs under the chair, his sneakers rubbing the carpet every time he did. "He sorta looks like me. More like you, though." He pointed to the picture. "That kid looks like me."

"That's his son."

Sammy didn't say anything.

"He does look like you."

154

"Think we could stay with him?"

"I don't know, Sam."

He shook his head. "I don't think so."

"Why?"

He pointed again to the picture. "Look."

"Yeah?"

"They got all nice clothes and stuff. We don't. And besides, she's not our mom."

"I don't know, Sam. We'll just have to see. He's nice. Just be good and don't say stupid stuff."

"I'm not stupid," he said, then looked at me. "He talks sorta like you, too. Pretty weird." Sam stood up, walking to the window. "This place is scary."

I nodded. "It's supposed to be."

"What do you have to do to get here?"

"Kill people and stuff. Drugs, too."

"That guy you beat up was a drug guy," he said matter-of-factly. "He should be here."

"Probably."

He studied the yard outside. "Do girls come here?"

"I don't know. Probably."

"He said Mom was in a corrections place."

"Yeah."

"Is that jail?"

I nodded.

"Has Mom ever been here?"

"No."

"She's bad like that guy, huh?"

"No. She's sick, Sam. That's all."

"I wish she'd get better."

"So do I."

"How long do we have to be here?"

"I don't know."

Sammy looked at me. "You don't wanna talk, do you?"

"Not really. I'm thinking."

"About what?"

"Stuff."

"What stuff?"

I sighed. "I don't know, Sam. Just stuff. No worries, huh? We'll be fine."

"I'm scared."

"Why?"

He shrugged. "Just am. I don't want to go home, but I don't want to stay here. What if they put me in there?" He pointed to the yard.

"Why would they, Sam?"

" 'Cause I hit the sheriff. He coulda died."

"He didn't, though," I said. "And besides, you're too young. They don't put kids here."

"Well, I still don't like it here, and I don't want to go home."

I didn't have anything to say to that, and Sam didn't press it. I didn't want to go home, either.

Chapter Seventeen

*T*en minutes later, Samuel came back in and sat down behind his desk. "You had enough to eat?"

We nodded. Sammy piped up. "Pretty good for jail food. I always thought it was bread and water."

He laughed. "Well, maybe a long time ago, Sam, but not now." He straightened a few things on his desk, then folded his hands together. "I've made a few calls."

My heart jumped.

He looked at me. "I know what happened at your school, Ian. Mr. Florence has a broken jaw and has filed charges against you." He paused. "There was also an incident involving a county sheriff just north of here." He leveled his eyes at me. "He was assaulted, his firearm taken from him and his radio disabled." His expression turned to stone. "I'm going to be blunt. Do you know anything about this?"

My heart sank. I nodded.

He sighed. "Thank you for your honesty. Your pictures were furnished to the sheriff, and though he couldn't identify Sammy, he identified you."

"Our pictures? How?"

"I read a communiqué on the assault after it happened, and when you showed up today, I had a suspicion, based on the officer's description of the perpetrator, that it was you. It struck me as more than a coincidence given your circumstances and the route you must have taken. You traveled down through that county." He looked at me and could tell I was confused. "You were photographed as you came into the prison. Everybody is. I faxed the pictures to the sheriff's office while you were eating."

My heart sank, and the picture I had of him, even tarnished, dulled to the point of nothingness. To him, we were the same as everybody else in this place. "So now what?"

He could see it in my eyes. "Ian, you've got to understand the position I'm in. I want to help you, but I'm constrained by the law. I *am* the law."

I looked at my feet.

"I've spoken to the sheriff, and with you under my guardianship, he'll drop the charges."

I looked at him. "You'd do that?"

He half smiled, almost painfully. "I can't say that I trust you, Ian. You've been through a lot and you've committed two serious crimes, but I have a responsibility to you as your father, and I want to see you get on track."

I bit back a remark he wouldn't appreciate. "Under your guardianship? What does that mean?"

"It means that if you do anything illegal, I'm responsible for you; any damages you cause and any restitution to be paid falls on me. The same goes for Sammy."

Sammy's eyes brightened. "Does that mean you'll be our dad?"

Our father looked like he'd just been stabbed through the

heart with a wooden stake, and while it killed me that Sammy would wear something so pitiful on his sleeve, I liked seeing the pain in our father's eyes. He deserved every ounce of it. "I am your father, Sammy, but it means things legally that you don't have to worry about right now."

"Oh." He sat back.

I still wasn't sure what was going on, but I did understand why he was doing what he did. He had to. But it didn't make things easier to swallow. "It just happened," I said. "It was raining and we were tired and everything just went down so fast. I talked to Sammy about it, and I know it shouldn't have happened, but it did."

Sammy cut in. "He told me the guy was just doing his job and that I shouldn't have whacked him."

Samuel nodded. "That's good, Sammy. You shouldn't have. We have laws in this country for a reason, and we must obey them. If you don't"—he gestured to the prison yard—"you end up here, and we don't want that."

I glowered at him, defensive. "Is that what you tell your kids when they screw up? That they'll end up here?"

He backtracked. "I have spoken to them about this place, and I'm not making a distinction between you and anybody, Ian. You are no different from my other children."

I saw the look in his eyes that told the real truth, and the killer of it was that I understood. He had a new life, just like I wanted one. But it still made me mad. "Except that they have someplace to sleep."

He winced, and his jaw muscles worked. "You made choices, Ian—"

"Don't talk to me about choices. You have no idea."

"I know your mother is sick, but—"

I leveled a stare at him. "But what? What do you know about my life?"

Sammy kicked his feet under the chair, still looking around and uncomfortable with the tone of things. "Ian says you go here if you kill people or sell drugs. Mom is sick 'cause of drugs, so drug guys should be there." He pointed outside. "Like the one Ian beat up."

Samuel raised his eyebrows.

I shook my head. "He wouldn't let us see Mom." I stared at him. "The *law* wasn't there to make everything all better. Sorry."

He steepled his fingers under his chin. "Have you had anger-management counseling, Ian?"

I shook my head. "I guess I was too busy doing your job to worry about that."

He ignored the jab. "You seem to have a propensity for violence."

"I have a propensity for wanting to be left alone."

He softened his look. "I'm concerned about that."

"Why now?"

"Ian, I know how you must feel—"

I interrupted. "No, you don't. You have no idea how I feel. You left, remember? You were the one who couldn't handle it, right? She's an addict! God, Dad, I'm not stupid, so don't treat me like it. And don't sit there and pretend you give a crap about us." Tears were hot and wet on my cheeks, and I wiped them away, pissed because he was sitting there like his concern was real and pissed because I was screwing it up by being pissed. I took a breath. "I don't need anger-management anything. I know I shouldn't have hit Coach Florence and I know I hurt him, but he

160

shouldn't have grabbed me. I was leaving, anyway, just like they wanted."

"He touched you?"

I nodded. "He swung me around, so I hit him. He's hated me since school started."

He took a deep breath. "Okay. Let's start by not assuming things about each other. I won't assume what you've gone through and what has happened, and you won't assume I don't have an idea of what a tough life is. Everybody goes through struggle, Ian."

I studied him, thinking about the offer and desperately wanting to get back on track. "Deal."

"I've talked to your case worker and the district attorney in Spokane. Nobody can locate your mother, and Child Protective Services has found clear neglect and child endangerment. Their ruling will remove you from the house and your mother's custody until she is deemed fit to have custody. The DA is pushing hard with the assault charges filed by the school and the teacher you hit." He frowned. "Unfortunately, Ian, this is just as much political as anything. These types of crimes are a hot spot right now, and the school needs to set an example."

"I was taking care of Sam just fine."

He shook his head. "Well, apparently the individual who called in the report felt strongly enough to do it personally."

"What does that mean?"

He furrowed his brow. "It means that usually when a teacher or administrator finds reason to believe that neglect, abuse, or child endangerment is present, they go through the school counselor, and the counselor then takes it from there. This person didn't."

161

I looked at him and could tell he thought something was strange about it. "Ms. Veer?"

"I wasn't told who."

"She told me . . . ," I started, then stopped. Ms. Veer had helped the way she thought was best.

"She told you what?"

"Nothing. It all started with her, I guess. She came to the house."

He nodded. "The report says the individual saw evidence of drug use, and upon questioning, Sammy told her that along with your mother not having been home for two weeks, drug use was prevalent when your mother was home." He looked at me seriously. "You sleep in a shed when this happens?"

I shrugged. "Not like we could rent a room at the Hilton, right?"

"I'm sorry."

I brushed it off, unable to get the bitterness off my tongue. "So what does that mean? The charges?" I said, glancing at Sammy. He gave me a guilty look.

"It means that with the circumstances surrounding the charges, and your mother's disappearance, the state has mandated the charges be upheld and that removal is necessary."

"Remove us from what? Her? She's never home, anyway."

He nodded. "You know what I'm saying."

"So what do we do?" I asked.

He stood. "We get things fixed. We have to find your mother and get her into treatment, if at all possible. Not just for the sake of having a clean mother," he said with a sad look, "but for her, too." He walked to the door, picking up our packs along the way. "This isn't a good place for children. I'll have Jannette begin the paperwork and we'll get you taken care of."

I couldn't believe it. He was helping. Taking care of things. Maybe we could be in that picture after all. Sammy and I walked into the reception area. Jannette wasn't there, so Dad opened the door to the corridor.

Four guards in blue uniforms waited in the hall.

I turned. "What . . . ?"

He looked at me. "You're wanted on a felony warrant for assault on your teacher, Ian. I have to have you and Sammy transported back to Spokane to face those charges."

"I thought . . ."

He held his hand out to the guards, who inched forward when I stepped back. "Hold off, guys." They stood down, and he shook his head. "There's no other way, Ian. I'm sorry."

I knew then that this was the end. He'd do what he could from a distance, but nothing had changed. He wouldn't follow through with Mom. No rehab. No nothing. "So you're arresting me."

There was a pleading look in his eyes, but also an edge to his mouth. I knew he was afraid I'd fight. "No, I'm not. I'm transporting you. That's all. It has to be done this way, Ian, and I wish I could change that, but I can't. The state patrol was going to pick you up, but I pulled some strings, and you'll be taken back by my guys. No handcuffs, no rough treatment—just a ride in a bus."

I looked at Sammy, then back to our father. The pressure rose in my chest, and I felt that tightness flushing my neck. Our father knew what Sammy was going back to. "There's no way he can stay with you?"

He looked at Sammy, standing filthy and dejected against the wall. He took a breath. "No. He has to be processed, and—"

I shook my head. "Forget it." I held my hand out to Sammy, and he took it. "Let's go, Sam."

163

As we started down the corridor, Samuel called to us. "You'll be well taken care of, and so will Sammy. I'll make sure of it." He paused. "I'll be in Spokane soon."

I looked at him there in the middle of the hall. All this only to be taken back to the thing I ran from. "Liar."

They took us down flights of stairs this time, skipping the elevator, and we walked out, taking a right and trudging around the corner of the building. Past that and down a short walkway, we came to some kind of transport area where a short bus, painted gray, waited for us as its engine idled. A guard stood by the door. Another sat at the wheel.

As we left the four guards and boarded, I heard one of them tell the guard waiting by the bus door that he should be careful. "Warden's kids, Iggy. Be nice."

The other one nodded.

Sammy and I sat next to each other midway back. The guard stood next to the driver as the doors closed. Short and stocky with a gut hanging over his belt, he glared at me. Both he and the driver were unarmed, and I assumed it was because this was a minimum-security transport. "Your butt leaves that seat, I don't care whose kid you are."

I stared at him.

He walked down the aisle. "When I speak to you, I expect an affirmative answer." He leaned into my face, a can of pepper spray in his hand. *Do you understand me, son?*

I looked at him and felt his breath on my face and almost hoped he'd do something, because pepper spray or not, I'd bend him into a pretzel. Then my father would have something to cuff me for.

Sammy remained silent, not meeting the guard's eyes. I couldn't keep mine from his.

"You going to be a tough guy? You just try it," he said, backing down the aisle and taking his seat near the driver as he threw our packs down. "Let's go, Lou."

Chapter Eighteen

And we went. We covered miles in minutes that had taken hours to walk, and the bare landscape, dreary and sullen and bleak, zipped by. Our dad could have taken us himself, and I had a dull ache inside that told me that if he'd really wanted it, Sammy could have stayed. I stared out the window for an hour, and as the scrub turned to farmland and the rocks turned to waving sheets of green wheat and checkerboard squares of tilled land, I didn't see many options left for us.

Nobody could find our mother, and I didn't believe Samuel McDermott would try to locate her like he said. He wouldn't be in Spokane, either. We were on the road to exactly what I'd run from, and Samuel McDermott might try to help us, but it would be the same kind of help Ms. Veer would have given. By the rules and at a distance. Sammy would be placed in some sort of institution or foster home, I would be in juvie, and Samuel McDermott could sit on his deck sipping iced tea while his other kids played, thinking he'd done everything he could for us. He'd pay for a lawyer and talk on the phone to people and write letters until it was over. He'd oversee our hell, and my little brother would get everything he needed except for a dad who gave a crap about us.

I watched the land roll by and wondered if being out there again, starving and wet and cold and homeless, would be better. It wouldn't. We couldn't run. Coach Schmidt was right. There was nothing out there for us but bad news, and I felt trapped. I'd also realized, when I'd looked into my father's eyes as he'd shipped us off, that feeling sorry for myself wouldn't do a thing but make me weak, and I'd felt sorry for myself since day one. My life, our lives, were what we made them. Samuel McDermott or not, I was Ian McDermott, and the way I saw life was the way I'd live life.

A ways into the trip, I realized the only thing that could help would be having Mom back. We had to find her. I had to get her into rehab, and she needed to take care of Sammy. I knew for a fact that when she wanted to be found, the only one who could find her was me. I could talk to her. I could get her into rehab. Any cop or judge or counselor would end up with a whole lot of nothing if they tried to track her down, because with my mom, out of sight was out of mind. She'd let it all slide unless I was there to push her into it.

We needed to get off this bus. Escape didn't seem too likely unless I took out the asshole with the gut and the wicked smile, but I didn't want another assault charge, even though it wouldn't bug me a bit to feel his face against my fist. One look at him and you knew he was a power tripper. He liked hurting people. I didn't figure it would be illegal if we did escape, either. We hadn't been officially detained by the police or the court, and Samuel even said I wasn't being arrested. We were simply being shipped home by our dad, and it just happened to be a prison bus taking us there. If we could get out, we could find Mom.

I looked over my shoulder. The emergency exit had some

167

sort of device on it. No dice there. We did have the bathroom option or the sick option, but I figured they wouldn't let us both off the bus at the same time. The only way out was to get past the guards, and I wanted to do it without another assault charge. Unless, of course, they got off the bus first.

I wondered what they would do if we did take a pit stop, and I couldn't imagine the guard following us off the bus. He'd get off first to make sure we didn't make a break for it. My hope was that the driver, after three hours of having his butt on the seat, would take a stretch, too. I nudged Sammy. "Say you have to go to the bathroom really bad."

"Huh?"

"Do it, Sam. We've got to find Mom."

He perked up, then raised his hand. Iggy laughed, shaking his head. "This ain't a classroom, little boy. What do you have to say?"

"I have to go."

"You can wait."

He shook his head. "I can't."

Iggy looked to Lou, then Lou nodded. "We're five minutes from a rest stop. You can wait until then."

Five minutes later, we exited the highway and rolled up to a rest area. I slowly took the map out of my backpack, careful not to catch Iggy's attention, and stuffed it in my back pocket. Lou cut the engine and stood, stretching his back. Evil Iggy stood at the door.

Sammy and I both stood.

Iggy shook his head, pointing to me. "You stay."

"I have to go, too."

"One at a time. The boy goes first, then you."

"He can't go if he's scared. I have to go with him."

Iggy smiled. "That ain't my problem."

168

"It will be if I tell my dad you made him go in his pants."

He hesitated.

"I'll tell him you threatened me with pepper spray, too." I smiled. "They got shit duty at the prison? I'll make sure you get it."

Lou cut in. "They ain't inmates, Iggy. Ease up." He stuck an unlit cigarette in his mouth. " 'Sides, the kid is right. Warden'll chew your ass big."

Iggy stared daggers at me, then nodded. "Three minutes."

I took Sammy's hand, leading him toward the mini-mart and hoping the restrooms would be around the corner. They were. As we rounded it, I stopped. "Let's go."

Sammy looked around. "Where?"

I looked to the east. "Come on." We started running, staying in line with the building as long as we could before a rock outcrop changed our direction. I looked back as we came in the line of sight of the bus, and heard shouts. Then Iggy and Lou were running after us. "Faster, Sam. Come on."

Outrunning Iggy and Lou would have been a snap for me, but Sammy was slow. And tired. He kicked his legs as fast as he could, but they gained on us. I turned to look back and Iggy was leaving Lou behind, his stumpy legs pistoning under his bouncing gut. If he kept it up, he'd catch us.

We ran. The field was tilled and rutted and the going rough. Sammy's legs were giving out. Lou faltered after a couple hundred yards, slowing to a jog, but Iggy kept it up, huffing and puffing after us with surprising wind. I wasn't going back to that bus, and I knew Iggy would get his licks in good and hard before cuffing me, so I made a decision.

"Keep going, Sam. Don't give up. You can't." I had a feeling I could take care of Iggy if I needed to, and I would if Sammy couldn't go farther, but I didn't want another "anger management"

169

episode that left some power-tripping asswipe lying in a field wondering what had hit him and a bunch of administrators talking about my propensity for violence. We had to outrun him.

Sammy kept it up, and Iggy finally gave in after a couple of minutes, stopping in the middle of the field and putting his hands on his knees as he caught his breath. We kept on until they were out of sight, then slowed to a fast walk for another ten minutes. Sammy kicked a dirt clod. "Now we're really in trouble. Run, run, run; get in trouble. That's all it ever is. And besides that, our boards are on the bus. Now we'll never get them back."

We came across a rotted log and sat down. I ruffled his hair. "I guess sometimes you've got to get in a little more trouble to get out of trouble, you know? Just like that guy Jacob said. And don't sweat the boards. We'll get new ones."

He slumped his shoulders. "Why did he send us back? He's our dad."

I shrugged. "I don't know, Sam. But things aren't that bad, and we'll make it better. I promise."

"Find Mom?"

I stood. "Yep." We walked until we topped a rise and saw a dirt road running east. It seemed familiar as we stumbled down to it, so I pulled the map from my pack and read it as we walked. "I think we're near that first town we came to, Sam."

"So?"

"So we're near Mr. Phillips's house." I remembered him cooking breakfast for us and him talking about his wife and the blisters on my hands after working so hard. My spirits rose. "We're going to his house."

"You know where?"

I looked at the map, trying to remember. "I think so. Come on."

We headed west, then cut up north at another dirt road, and three hours later, just as the sun slid behind the hills, we found his road, turning west and walking for another hour. In the twilight, I recognized his mailbox. We headed up his drive, dirty and dead-dog tired.

A single light burned in what I knew was the kitchen, and when I knocked, lights turned on in a row toward the door. He greeted us with a rifle in his hands and slippers on his feet. "Mr. Phillips?"

He squinted, then lowered the rifle. "Well, I be damned." He looked us up and down. "You boys look like hell."

I stood awkwardly.

"Come on in." He led us to the kitchen, where a pot of coffee, a half-eaten sandwich, and a bowl of soup sat lonely on the table. A baseball game crackled from the radio next to the toaster, the tinny voice of the announcer bouncing off the faded linoleum.

Mr. Phillips didn't ask the usual questions, and I was glad for it. He told us we were hungry by the looks of it and opened the refrigerator, motioning for me to get sandwich stuff out. Five minutes later, Sammy and I were putting the lids on roast beef sandwiches and spooning soup into bowls. Mr. Phillips waited for us to eat, and we sat around the table together, chewing and gulping and smacking our lips. "I suppose," he said, "that the only reason you're here is that you have nowhere else to go." He raised his wrinkled eyelids to me. "You're in a heap of trouble, aren't you, boy?"

I nodded. "We have to get to Spokane."

"Dad didn't turn up?"

I shook my head.

He smiled sadly. "Didn't turn up the way you figgered, then."

"He's got his life," I said.

"Ain't that the way of it nowadays."

"I guess so."

"You need a lift to town."

"Yes."

"Too late tonight."

"We can sleep in the barn if you'd like."

He shook his head. "My boy's room is down the hall on the left. You take it."

"Thank you."

He shrugged. "Ain't been slept in since he left."

"He doesn't come around very much?"

He smiled. "He's got his own life."

I smiled back. "I guess that's the way it is."

"Guess it is." He stood, clearing his dishes. "I'm up early. Sunrise. We'll get some chow and get you on the road."

"The police are looking for us, Mr. Phillips."

He put his hand on my shoulder. "You live as long as me, some things are more clear than others, boy. Don't you worry about that."

Sammy and I cleared our own plates and did the dishes, finding the proper places for them and wiping the counters before we found the room. When I opened the door, I could tell things hadn't been touched in years. I could see from the lack of dust on all the furniture that Mr. Phillips cleaned every once in a while, but I felt like I was entering a museum.

Several trophies with animals depicted on them were planted

on one windowsill, and 4-H ribbons dotted the wall around them. The bedspread was checked blue and red, and the wood floors creaked when I stepped inside. Both of us were dead tired, and we fell onto the bed without taking our clothes off. Sammy was asleep in minutes, his breathing easy, and I was asleep soon after, my belly full and a ride to Spokane planned for the next morning. At least some things could be normal, and I didn't mind one bit taking the place of Mr. Phillips's son for the night.

I woke up wishing I could stay with Dunbar Phillips forever. We could work from sunup to sundown and eat good food and talk and listen to stories and not have to see a single soul in the whole world unless we wanted to. I could carry on what Mr. Phillips's son hadn't, and I wondered what kind of idiot would pass up the opportunity. I decided his son must be crazy.

I rubbed the sleep from my eyes and walked to the hall, where I found two bath towels folded on a small table near the bathroom. The bathroom was plain white tile with blue lines and nothing else but a bar of soap on the sink, a medicine cabinet, and a hand towel hanging from a hook on the wall.

I took a shower, washing away the grime from over a week of running, standing under the water and watching streams of dirty water swirl down the drain. I scrubbed every part of me three times, and with the towel wrapped around my waist, woke Sammy up and hustled him under the steaming water. It was the only time I could remember that he didn't complain about getting cleaned up, and I almost wished he would.

Fifteen minutes later, we arrived in the kitchen to find Mr. Phillips cooking breakfast. He mumbled directions and pointed vaguely to the cupboards, sipping coffee while he flipped eggs. I set the table, and Sammy poured three glasses of milk and got the bread down for me to toast. Mr. Phillips asked if we slept well and didn't say much else, sticking to the task at hand, until he told me he'd been a short-order cook when he was twenty.

"I could cook for a whole tribe and not get an order wrong," he said, sliding eggs onto plates and setting them on the table. "Met my wife there, as a matter of fact. The Cascade Café, it was."

"Really?"

He nodded, pouring me a cup of coffee and sitting. "Belgian waffle, one egg sunny-side up, and a glass of apple juice."

"She liked that the best?" I said.

He looked at his plate, his hands to either side of it. "That's what she ordered the first time I ever saw her." He picked up a fork, holding off on his eggs. "I cooked that for her fifty-three times."

"Fifty-three?"

"On the morning of every anniversary we ever celebrated, plus the first time. Fifty-two plus one."

"You loved her a lot," Sammy said. They were the first words he'd spoken since waking.

He chuckled. "Ain't much more to a man like me than the woman who'll put up with him for half a century." He looked at us. "She woulda liked you boys."

"I'm sorry."

He cut an egg, shaking his head. "Nothing to be sorry about, Ian. Her time came, and we'll be together again soon enough."

Sammy took a drink of his milk. "Did she stay home all the time?"

Mr. Phillips nodded.

Sammy put his head down and ate his eggs.

A knock at the door broke up our conversation. I glanced at the clock, and it was seven-thirty. Mr. Phillips stood, peeking out the window. "Sheriff's here."

My chest tightened, the fear of having been double-crossed clutching at my chest.

Mr. Phillips walked to the front door, and I followed, staying back behind the corner of the wall and listening. He opened the door. "Howdy, Mort."

"Hello, Dunbar," the voice said.

"What can I do for you?"

"Got a call in for two runaways. Troublemakers. Got the boys out looking for them on account of a heap of shit they been into, and I'm canvassing houses, making sure everybody's okay."

"That so?"

"Sure is. Seems they escaped a prison transport, of all things. Say the older one is dangerous. Fifteen ain't dangerous in my book, but you never know these days. You seen anything like that lately?"

"Nope."

"No boys runnin' loose?"

"Can't say I have, Mort."

"Put a call in if you do?"

"Sure thing." Mr. Phillips said goodbye and shut the door, watching the sheriff get in his car and leave. He laughed. "You boys got everybody in a muddle."

I looked at him. "Thank you."

He smiled. "Gets a might boring around here anyway."

I followed him to the kitchen, where we cleared plates.

"You got something waiting for you in Spokane?" he said.

"Our mom. We have to find her."

He looked at Sammy. "People are given a certain thing in life, I think. Difference between the bad and the good is what you do with it."

"We need to help her."

He nodded. "We'll get you to Spokane so you can do just that."

Chapter Nineteen

The ride into town was mostly silence. Sammy still didn't talk, just stared at his feet or out the window, and it worried me. I didn't ask him what the matter was, because I knew. This whole thing was finally getting to him. It had hurt to see him in our dad's office, because for all his being slow, he understood what was said. He'd put all his hopes on the idea that somehow things would be new and better when we found him, and that just hadn't been the case.

Mr. Phillips respected the silence, and I was glad for it because I didn't want to talk. It was embarrassing thinking about him knowing anything about our lives, and I didn't want him to know our past or that Mom was the way she was. I wanted him to think we were good.

The minutes slipped past, and I couldn't help but glance out the mirrors every so often looking for cops. Mr. Phillips noticed and told us to duck if we saw one. I didn't know exactly what we were heading into, but I figured Bernie's, the tavern Mom went to, wouldn't be open at eight-thirty in the morning. I decided we'd start where we last saw her. Malachi's house.

Mr. Phillips drove us to Malachi's block, and I could almost feel the unease coming from the old man as we drove deeper into the neighborhood. I looked around and saw cars on blocks and garbage in weed-filled yards and paint peeling from houses and wished I'd told him to drop us farther up the hill.

"You sure you want me to drop you 'round here?" he said.

I nodded. "Home sweet home."

He glanced at me. "I suppose a boy like you can take care of yourself."

I told him to stop the truck. Malachi's house was around the corner. I hopped out, then helped Sammy jump down. "Thank you, Mr. Phillips."

He nodded. "You take care of your family, boy. I know you can."

"I will." Both Sammy and I waved until the truck was out of sight. I looked around at all the things I'd wanted to leave behind forever, and my chest felt hollow. I'd never wanted to see this again. The people. The way. The life.

I realized that they were all right. Coach Schmidt, Bennie, Mr. Phillips, and our father. Nobody could be what they weren't, and I'd tried to run from it instead of making it better. God or whatever was up there made things a way for a reason. I couldn't get away from this. I couldn't get away from what we were and what we'd done, and the reasons why didn't matter. But I could fight. I could do exactly what Dunbar Phillips said. I could fight for what I had, and I could try to make it right.

Malachi probably hadn't seen the world before noon for the last twenty years, and as Sammy and I walked the rest of the way to his house, I was hoping he'd still be crashed. One look at a scumbag like him and you knew he'd been sucking meth into his body for years, and I guessed if I caught him by surprise, I wouldn't have a problem getting what I wanted. I'd dealt with wasted addicts trying to jack me up on the street, and I knew they folded when things turned against them. Unless they had a gun.

After Mr. Phillips was gone, I turned to Sam. "You stay here, okay? And if you hear anything bad at all, sirens or yelling or anything, run to Blind Man Thompson's house. He'll take care of you."

He looked at me with wide eyes, then shook his head. "I don't want you to go, Ian. Really. I don't even want her to be my mom anymore. We could just go live with Mr. Phillips."

"We have to do this, Sam. You just stay here and everything will be fine. I'll find out where Mom is and we'll get her." I ruffled his hair, and before he could argue anymore, I turned around and walked. "I'll be back. Don't worry."

I rounded the corner, keeping my eye on the house as I approached. Malachi had visitors. Two cars sat in the driveway, and one of them wasn't good news at all. Chopped, lowered, and gleaming metallic black, a brand-new Cadillac Escalade sat in the driveway. Twenty-four-inch Enkei wheels with Yokohama rubber wrapping around the wicked things made the truck a diamond sitting in the crap pile of a neighborhood around it.

I was smart enough to know that a tricked-out truck like that sitting in front of a dump of a house meant one thing. It belonged to a supplier, not a pusher, and I also knew enough about guys like that to know there'd be a gun in there, too. The pieces fell together for me then; Malachi wasn't just an addict, he was a pusher, and that meant he had connections.

If I'd had any street sense at all, I'd have turned my butt

around and walked away. Pushers were one thing because they were usually so strung out that the only thing they could do was measure dope and count cash, but the suppliers were different. They ran the operations and the girls, and most weren't users. They were the corporate gunslingers of the drug world, and they played for keeps.

I weighed my options for a minute or so, the clock ticking in my head. I didn't want to go face to face with a dealer. Nobody in their right mind did. We needed my mom, though. I couldn't go back, and there were no options left. I had to do this.

I made my way to the neighbor's yard, then slipped between the houses, peeking in the side windows. Near the rear of the house, I peered in and saw Malachi sleeping on a ratty couch, sprawled out, with his arm hanging to the floor and his mouth wide open.

I watched for a minute or so, then made my way around the corner to the backyard, stepping to the back door. I looked through the cracked window of the door and saw an empty kitchen, filthy dirty and piled high with dishes, McDonald's wrappers, and garbage. I tried the knob, and it wiggled under my hand, the screws loose. It wasn't locked. Inside, I stopped, listening. Nothing.

As I crept through the kitchen, my heart beat thunder in my ears, and I wondered if I'd be able to hear anybody if they jumped me. Then it wouldn't matter. Nothing would. I took a right from the kitchen and found myself in a narrow hall, the room where Malachi slept in front of me. The door was cracked open, and I looked in. Still sleeping.

When Malachi's eyes exploded open, I was kneeling over him, my hand clamped hard over his mouth and my elbow digging a hole in his throat. He struggled wildly for a second until I jammed my elbow further against his throat. He stopped moving, his yellowed eyes panicked. I whispered, "Make a sound, and I'll do it, man. I swear to God, I'll crush it."

He blinked, trying to nod.

"Where is she?" I said. He stared at me, my hand still clamped over his mouth, and tried to talk. I looked into his eyes and wondered if I could risk letting him talk. If he yelled, I was dead. I kept my hand over his mouth, and my mind raced. "Okay, here's the deal. You yell, and I'm dead, right?" He smiled under my hand. I clamped tighter, digging my elbow further into his neck. "I know I'm dead, too. But you'll be dead about two seconds after me, because I'll tell them you're the guy who told me where to steal their stuff and that we're splitting it."

I let that sink in for a minute, and he got it. If anything was certain death around here, it was being a snitch. I loosened my elbow a little. "You understand?"

He nodded.

I took my hand from his mouth. "Where is she?"

He sneered, his voice hoarse and low. "He'll kill you."

"You heard what I said, man. I'll snitch you out, and you know what'll happen."

He smiled. "She's upstairs. With him. Go ahead, boy. Go get her."

Things had just gotten more complicated. I thought about Sammy outside, and I knew that if I made a break for it, we could probably get away. For now. They'd catch up to me, though, and that would be it. I looked around the room for something to tie Malachi up with, but there was nothing. My elbow was still jammed against his neck. "I'm going up there, and you're going to go back to sleep, understand? Like you don't know anything." I paused, and the smell of his breath hit me. Rancid and sick. "I'll tell him, man. I'll tell him it was you."

He snorted. "You're a dead man walking. I don't need to do a damn thing."

I stood.

"He owns her, boy."

I walked out.

I thought again about leaving as I crept down the hall to the stairs. The anger returned as I reached them. If it was just me, I'd leave. I'd go and live my life and forget she ever existed. She should be doing this for us, not the other way around, and I hated her for it. But Sammy needed her. I needed her. The only problem was that I didn't want to need her. I didn't want to *know* her.

I started up the stairs, careful for creaks, and stopped at the top, listening for any sound. For all I knew, Malachi would start yelling. To my right was another bathroom, and beyond that, three more bedrooms. The first one on my left had the door closed.

I turned the knob slowly, opening the door a crack. I couldn't see anything. Opening it wider, the bed came into view. On it lay my mom. Alone. My heart skipped a beat.

I turned and had just enough time to see the blur of a black fist holding a pistol screaming toward my head. The pistol grip connected with my temple, and then I blacked out.

When I came to, I was lying on the floor and my mother was screaming. She was in the hall, on the ground, and fighting with the guy who'd hit me, her arms and legs flailing as she hysterically screamed that he'd killed her son. Me.

The guy straddled my mother on the floor, his fists pistoning on her face. I staggered to my feet and noticed his pistol lying on the floor, dropped during the struggle. The man beating her was oblivious to everything except for his fists connecting with her face, and as I wrapped my forearm around his neck from behind and jammed the pistol behind his ear, he stopped. I cocked it just like I'd seen on TV.

I yanked him off my mother and he fell back, swiveling on his butt to face me. My mother rose, staring at me as I pointed the gun at the man. I stepped forward, looked at my mother's bloody face, then stared at him. "Don't ever touch her again."

I nodded to her. "Go downstairs."

She did, running down the stairs as she wiped the blood from her ruined face. The man sat still, staring at me, his eyes white and calm against his dark skin. Even with the gun in my hand, warm from his own hand, I felt like I was no match for him. "I didn't want trouble, mister. My brother needs her, and that's all."

His face was impassive, his bullet head shining with sweat. "You screwed with the wrong people, kid."

I stepped past him, to the stairs. "I didn't screw with anybody. I just needed my mom."

He stared at me for a moment, then looked at the gun. "She belongs to me."

I shook my head. "She's going to get clean. And you don't own her."

He smiled, totally and completely relaxed. Powerful. "You've got balls, kid. You're the one who jacked Malachi up last week, aren't you?"

I nodded. "Tell him to stay away from us or he'll get more of the same."

He studied me for a moment, then nodded. "You look me up

if you need a job, huh? Your mother owes me, and as far as I see it, you just took on the debt."

I nodded, then surprised myself. I held the pistol out to him. "I told you I don't want trouble. Just her."

He took it, released the hammer, and waved it at the stairs. "Get, then."

Chapter Twenty

I met Mom downstairs, where she'd taken an old shirt from the sofa and was dabbing her face. Malachi was nowhere to be found. "Ian . . ."

"Come on." I walked to the front door and waited. She cast her eyes down and walked out. I met her in the yard. "Sammy's waiting around the corner. He needs your help." We were walking across the yard when Malachi rushed out the door and ran down the steps, an ugly and fearful smear on his face.

I squared myself in front of him, ready, when he jolted to a stop ten feet away. He pulled a revolver from his waistband and pointed it at me. Just then, Dunbar Phillips's old pickup screeched around the corner and skidded to a halt in front of the house, making a racket as the tires skipped to a stop. Sammy sat in the passenger seat, craning his head out the window and yelling for us to come.

Malachi stood between us and the truck. I took a breath, staring at the gun. His hand shook. Then my mother stepped in front of me. "Don't do this, Malachi," she said. "It's not his fault."

"Shut your face, whore!" he snarled, cocking the gun.

She didn't move. The screen door behind us slammed shut. Malachi's eyes went from us to the porch. He smiled. "Now you're dead, boy."

"Leave off, Malachi," the voice, deep and strong, called out.

"But—" Malachi began.

"Leave off, dog!"

Malachi lowered the pistol.

I grabbed Mom's arm and we hustled past, opening the truck door and hopping in. Mr. Phillips gunned it, and the last thing I saw was the man on the porch, his outline dark and chiseled and dangerous, watching us go.

Mr. Phillips didn't know where he was going and I didn't really, either. He'd hung around after dropping us off because, he said, "I'm a crusty old bastard with nothing better to do." But we had Mom, I was alive, and now we could get the ball rolling. I still had three things to do before I turned myself in, though, the first being getting Mom to the rehab center at the hospital.

Mr. Phillips passed a small park, and I asked him to pull into the parking lot. I told Sammy to stay in the truck, then I got out, taking Mom's arm and walking her to a picnic bench under a maple tree. I sat down, ignoring the sight of her battered face. "You need to get clean."

She gave me a desperate look. "Ian . . ."

I shook my head. "Sammy's going to foster care today, and he'll be there until you are clean. There are no options here, Mom. None. And I'm not going to see him end up the way I am." I looked at her. "Or you. Do you understand? You *will* get cleaned up. You'll do what they say and go to hearings and do all the crap that you have to to get him back, or you'll never see us again. I swear to God, Mom, this is it. There's no other way."

Her lip trembled, and she raised her hand to my face. "Ian, baby, please, what happened?"

I took her hand away. *"I just told you!"* I grabbed her by the shoulders, and the urge to throttle her nearly overwhelmed me. "Sammy needs you! He's needed you for a long time, and you're going to ruin his life unless you straighten up! I'm taking you to rehab, and you'll stay there until you're clean, and then you'll get him back and take care of him."

She sobbed. "I can't, baby. I've tried. . . ."

"Just like you tried with Dad?" I shot at her. "Just like you tried when you were pregnant with Sam?" I let go of her. "Jesus, Mom, you made him the way he is! Don't you think you at least owe him this? I've taken care of him the best I know, but I can't anymore. He needs you, and he'll be lost if you don't do this. Please. I'm begging. Just stay in rehab long enough to think straight. You can do it if you want to."

She looked to the truck, then back to me. "I'll try." I nodded, and she touched my face again. "You're different now." Her fingers were soft against my cheek. "What happened?"

I shook her hand away and walked to the truck.

Chapter Twenty-One

Mr. Phillips followed my directions to the rehabilitation wing of the medical center, and I walked Mom inside. I'd tried to get her to go once before, but the deal was shot down on account of her leaving me standing at the front doors, watching her walk away.

Sammy hadn't said a word besides "hi" since she got in the truck, and he didn't react when she kissed him goodbye, just sat there looking at the stick shift with Mr. Phillips's wrinkled hand on it.

I walked out forty-five minutes later, tucking her admitting papers into my back pocket. She'd promised me she'd stay, and the only thing I could do was believe her. I didn't have any other options at this point, and by this time tomorrow, I'd be in juvie, locked up with all the other social retards in Spokane.

The temptation to ask Mr. Phillips to take Sammy until I turned myself in was strong, but I couldn't. He'd done enough already, and I didn't want to see him get into trouble for harboring a ten-year-old fugitive, which no doubt would constitute some type of terroristic action by an eighty-four-year-old man.

I asked him to drive back to our old neighborhood. Blind Man Thompson would take Sammy in until tomorrow, and by then, my business with Bennie, Principal Spence, and the list would be finished. I had to figure it out.

As we rounded the corner and I saw our house, I felt a pang of missing it. The hose and sprinkler Mrs. Vander had left on the porch were set up, the line snaking across the grass to a rainbow of water showering the half-green yard. No doubt Mrs. Vander had taken our absence as an opportunity to do it herself, and I realized it didn't make me mad. It made me want to do it myself.

Mr. Thompson sat in his rocker on his front porch, his cane resting across his knees as he stared at nothing. He had a Mariners cap cocked on his head, and aside from the slow rocking of the chair, he could have been a statue. I ushered Sammy from the truck and turned to our friend. "Thank you, Mr. Phillips."

The old man looked at me and smiled. "You take care of your family the way I seen you do and everything will be fine."

"I'll try."

He nodded. "Come for a visit anytime. I always got eggs." As he put the truck in gear, he looked to Sammy. "You buck up there, young man. You're a tough little cuss just like your brother, and I can see you love him just like he loves you. You do what he says and you'll be fine."

Sammy's lip trembled as he looked at Mr. Phillips, but he didn't cry. He clenched his teeth and nodded. "I will."

As Mr. Phillips drove off, I turned to Sammy. "You know what's going to happen, Sam, and you know what you have to do."

A tear slid down his cheek. "You're going away."

I nodded. "For a little while, yes. So are you. But we'll be back together. I promise."

His chest heaved. "I'm scared, Ian. I am. I just want to go home." He pointed to our house. "Just like it was before. We could skate and stuff, and I wouldn't complain when we had to sleep in the shed or anything. I'd try my hardest in school, too."

I knelt in front of him. "No, Sammy. We can't. And I don't want to. That's not good enough for us anymore. None of it is, and we're going to make it better."

"You'll come get me from that institutional thing you said?"

"I promise." I stood up and ruffled his hair. "Let's go."

Mr. Thompson smiled as we came up the stairs to the porch. "Thought you boys up and died."

"How'd you know it was us?" I said.

"Ain't deaf, just blind."

"Can Sammy stay with you until tomorrow?"

"Of course." He smiled, nodding my way. "You got business to attend to?"

I nodded, then remembered he was blind. "Yeah." I turned to Sammy, who sat on the steps. "I'll try to get here tomorrow, and we can do this together, Sam. Okay?"

"Promise?"

I thought about what I had to do. *The list.* "Yes, I promise."

He smiled. "Deal is a deal."

"No worries, buddy," I said, sitting next to him and giving him a hug. "I love you."

"Love you, too."

I stepped from the porch and began walking. I hadn't gone far when Sammy bolted down the stairs. "Hey, Ian! Mr. Phillips said I was tough, and I am! I'll be tough, okay? Just like you!"

"You are tough, and everything will be fine. We just have to make it work," I called. "Bye, Sammy."

"Bye."

I couldn't help it. I tried and tried, but by the time I'd rounded the corner, I was crying like a big fat baby. I wiped my eyes on my arm and felt the wind dry the sting from my eyes. I couldn't think about Sammy and what might happen. I had something to do, and it might be the shady way of getting myself straightened out, but I at least had one thing. A goal.

The list.

Chapter Twenty-Two

"You wounded me."

"Shut up, Ben."

He clutched his heart as we crouched near a hedge lining the administration building at the school. It was one-thirty in the morning, and we'd been scoping the place out for five minutes. "I'm hurt. You called that . . . that gorgeous girl with large breasts before you called me." He screwed his eyes up. "A grievous injury to my soul." He gave a dramatic sigh. "There you were, out on the road and skulking around deserted and lonely wilderness areas, and you think of her, not me. That, my friend, is true betrayal."

I rolled my eyes, peeking in the windows. "Sorry. You have hairy nipples."

"Now he insults my nipples. I should just go home."

"Be quiet. We're supposed to be quiet, remember? That means no casual conversation."

"Casual, he says. Maybe to you, but this assault on me is—"

"How are we getting in?" I said, deflecting his drama.

"Well, I figure we can either throw a brick through the window or use this," he said, digging in his pocket.

I looked in his hand. "You have a key?"

He nodded, admiring his shiny treasure. "Arguably the best way to enter a building unless you have access to explosives." He rubbed it between his fingers. "You just put it in and turn, and *bammo,* the door opens. Invented by the first man who built a house and couldn't get in."

"How did you get a key?"

He gave me a superior look. "How does one acquire a pimple? Some things just come naturally, Ian."

I stood. "Come on." We crept to the entrance facing the courtyard, and I glanced at the bell on its pedestal. Morrison must have won again, because it was turned upside down, no doubt a pint or so of Bennie's urine inside.

Bennie smiled. "It never gets old, you know?"

"Just open the door, Ben. I don't want to be here."

"You worry too much."

"Whatever. Come on."

Bennie slipped the key in the glass-and-metal door and turned it. No alarm. No sirens or beeping lights. I breathed a sigh of relief. Bennie opened the door, looking at the tension on my face. "No alarm systems. The district has to pay for football, remember?"

"Priorities," I said, stepping inside. The dim light from the trophy case, left on all night to keep Morrison High's treasures company, guided us down the hall to the office reception area, where Nurse Ratched had always given me my ration of crap about being late. Twenty feet farther and set dead center to the entrance was Principal Spence's office.

I tried the door, but it was locked. "Got a key for this one?" I whispered.

He smiled. "Human nature demands certain things, my man. Have you ever seen Spence walk down the hall?"

I nodded, nervous in the stillness of the empty building.

"What does he habitually do?"

"Twirls his keys on his finger. Get to the point."

"Have you ever counted the keys on his ring as he twirls?"

"No."

He shook his head as if I was a lost soul. "There're four keys on his ring. One for his Lexus, a house key, a key to the school, and another ignition key, for his wife's Infiniti. Nice car, too. Saw it once. A G20."

"So?"

"So he's a minimalist when it comes to keys. My dad is that way, too."

I waited.

He shook his head. "No key on his ring for this door."

I waited again.

He rolled his eyes. "Look in the pot, dummy."

I turned to the small potted tree next to the door, put my hand under the fake green moss-type stuff used to hide the soil, and pulled out a key. I looked at Ben. "You are incredible, Ben."

"It pays to pay attention. My dad's house key is in a pot next to our front door." He pointed to the door. "Spence unlocks in the morning and locks at night. My guess is that the extra key on his ring would upset the balance of his twirl."

I unlocked the door, and we were inside. The blinds were shut, so I closed the door and turned on the desk lamp perched next to the picture of his family. His computer, set on another desk to the side, glowed with the screen saver, which was a colorful portrayal of famous football plays drawn in the time-honored fashion of *X*'s and *O*'s intersected with lines.

Bennie sat at the desk, swiveling the chair to the computer. "If it's anywhere, it'll be here."

"You think he'd be that stupid?"

He laughed. "When you think you're God, it's impossible to think you're stupid."

I leaned over his shoulder as he worked the mouse, opening the document folder and browsing. Bennie began singing under his breath, and a couple of minutes later, he clicked on a document named "Woodcutter."

Bennie turned to me as the file loaded. "This is the only file in the directory that doesn't fit." He turned back, and a box blinked in the center of the screen, demanding a password. "Password protected," he said. "Somehow I don't think it's an account of Spence competing in the World Lumberjack Competition."

"So how do we find the password?"

He sat back, staring at the screen. "Most people put in familiar things so they can remember them, but there's too many with Spence, and we don't know him well enough. Crap."

I looked at the screen. "How many other things are there that need passwords?"

He returned to the keyboard, opening files left and right before he found what he wanted. "Five, including his Internet and intranet access. He probably has more, too. What are you getting at?"

I studied his desk. "They'd all be different passwords?"

Bennie shrugged. "Probably. If he's smart, they would be. Why?"

"You said yourself that people are creatures of habit." I remembered the key in the pot.

Bennie smiled. "Okey-dokey, then. I'll search the computer; you search the office. If he does have a list of passwords written down, they'd probably be within easy reach of his desk."

Bennie returned to the mouse, opening file after file while I searched the desk. No scraps of paper in the drawers, no slips hidden under the desktop mat, behind the family picture, or under the lamp. Then I saw the miniature bust of Thomas Jefferson. I tipped it back just as Spence might while sitting in his chair, and taped to the bottom were six passwords. "Bingo, Ben."

He turned. "My hero."

"Put them in and see, huh? I'm getting nervous."

"Righto, my partner in crime."

The "Woodcutter" file opened with the fourth password, which was "cleanup311," and we were greeted with what looked like a spreadsheet. Thirty-two names ran down the screen, with nearly half highlighted in red, and graphed across the page next to the names were numbers. There was no heading on the file or explanation of what the numbers were about, but I recognized some of the names.

"Hey, you're number thirteen," Bennie said. "This, my man, has to be the list."

I looked at it. Mine was highlighted red. "Yeah, but what is it?"

He turned to the screen. "Look," he said, running his finger down the line. "Mike Dupont, Sherry Magnuson, Jason Vervair, Yancy Robison, Naomi Holmes. All the reds are gone, man. Spence is highlighting everybody who's gone. Yancy went to the bad kids' school, Naomi transferred to that school for Native Americans, Mike Dupont dropped out, Sherry is at Kerner, and Jason was expelled."

"And I'm wanted by the police."

"Boo-hoo. Here's your list, man." Bennie clicked on the print button, and soon three copies were spitting out onto the desk.

"Yeah, but what do the numbers mean? There's percentages, too."

He scooped up the copies. "I don't know, but we got the goods, so we split now."

I looked at the computer. "Is there a way to erase the recent file log? I don't want him to know anybody was in here."

Ben nodded. "Good thinking, brainiac. Just a sec."

Chapter Twenty-Three

*F*ive minutes later, we were walking toward Bennie's house. I had the lists in my pocket but didn't know what to do with them. "Why?"

"I don't know, man. The numbers mean something, but obviously it's a hit list. Spence wants those guys out of the school, and the numbers will tell us why. That's my guess, anyway."

I took out the list and stopped under a streetlight. Across the page from the names were two numbers. The headings above those numbers were more numbers, the first being a *4* and the second a *7*. The next heading across the page was *WA*, and the last, near the right margin, was *FE*. I scanned down the numbers under the *4* heading. Most were under 70. Under the *7* heading, all were under 70.

Bennie turned around. "Uh, Ian? I know you're an outlaw and everything, but have you heard of a curfew? Standing under a streetlight at three in the morning isn't what good kids do."

I tucked the paper back in my pocket. "What do you think, Ben? Come on, you know everything."

He shrugged, lighting up a smoke. "I don't know, man. It could be all encoded or something."

"I've got to find out."

He exhaled. "Who do you know that might know, and do you trust that person?"

I thought about it for two seconds before Coach Schmidt came to mind. "Coach."

"The dyke?"

"Give it a rest, Ben. She's not that bad, and besides that, don't you think this whole 'I hate gay people' thing is old now?"

"Walk a mile in my shoes, Ian," he replied.

I spit on the sidewalk. "Bullshit, Ben. You *have* a dad."

"Don't think I haven't pondered what life would be like dead, Ian."

We'd talked about this the year before, and I thought he'd come to terms with things. "So you're going to kill yourself over it? Let them win?" I shook my head, watching him snuff his cigarette out under his heel. "Your dad may be different from most other dads, Ben, but he loves you. Maybe you should start appreciating it instead of feeling sorry for yourself all the time."

"So this is the hard talk that the best friend gives when things get out of hand?"

"Whatever you want to call it, man, but you're past that shit."

He smiled. "And you're in a position to set me straight?"

I glared at him. "I see you and what you have, Ben, and it doesn't have anything to do with me and what I have. You've helped me with everything you can, and I'm paying you back. That's what friends do. You've just got to see that after a while, nobody cares what you've been through or how tough things are. Coach Schmidt and Dunbar Phillips and even my dad showed me that. It's all up to you to do it."

He stared at the night sky, then lit up another smoke. "Easier said than done, Ian."

"Well, you're going to have to do it, Bennie. Sooner or later, anyway."

He laughed. "Jesus Christ Superstar talking from his garbage-can pulpit. Thanks but no thanks."

"Your choice."

Three silent blocks before Bennie's place, I dug the cell phone from my pocket and called Coach Schmidt. The battery was almost dead. "Coach?"

"Hello?"

"Coach. It's me, Ian."

"It's three-thirty," she said, sleep still in her voice.

"Not in China." I watched Ben watching for cops.

"Are you all right? What's wrong?"

"I'm back in town, and I need your help."

She paused. "I'll help you all I can, but—"

I cut in. "I broke into the school."

She sighed. "Ian, I can't help you this way. Please, you've got to understand—"

"I need your help. Really."

Silence. Then, "With what?"

"Will you meet us?"

"Now?"

"Yes."

"Are you in danger?"

"No. I'm turning myself in later, but I need you to look at something. Will you?"

"Where?"

"Fourteenth and Madison."

Silence, then, "I'll be there in twenty minutes."

As I stuffed the phone away, Bennie came over. "She take the bait?"

"Yes. Fourteenth and Madison in twenty minutes." I started walking. "She's on our side, Ben."

"Well, we'll see about that, huh? Fifty bucks says Fourteenth and Madison will be crawling with pigs in twenty minutes."

I kept walking. "I trust her."

"I don't."

"Then go home."

"No."

"Why not, Ben? You're all pissed at me now, anyway."

"So what? Just because you say stuff I don't like doesn't mean I hate you. I don't even really think you're wrong. I just don't like it."

"Me neither."

Fourteenth and Madison has a city park next to it, and we stood fifty feet into the darkness waiting for either cop cars or Coach Schmidt to arrive. No cops came, but a silver Toyota pickup truck rolled around the corner slowly. Bennie shook his head. "Chick in a truck. How stereotypical."

"Hey, you were wrong about the cops, so shut up."

"Yessir."

"Come on."

We walked to the street, and Coach Schmidt opened the passenger-side window. I nodded to her. "Thanks, Coach."

She looked at Bennie. "Where's Sammy?"

"Safe."

She nodded. "Hop in." We drove then, and as we wound our way to what I assumed was her house, Dwight Yoakam sang "Long White Cadillac" on the radio.

Bennie began singing along in his best sarcastic twangy voice while I filled Coach Schmidt in on our trip to Walla Walla and our father and all the garbage we'd gone through. Ben sang all the way through it.

"I get the picture, Ben." She changed the station. "What do I need to see, Ian?"

"Where are we going?"

"My apartment."

Bennie whistled. "Harboring a fugitive is a felony."

"So is strangling his best friend at four in the morning, so watch the sarcasm. We're not in school."

Ben widened his eyes at me. "Maybe you were right, Ian."

I turned to Coach Schmidt. "I need you to look at a list."

Chapter Twenty-Four

Coach Schmidt sat at the table in her kitchen, her big arms resting around the list as she studied it. Her brow furrowed, and she remained silent. Bennie sipped a Pepsi while I ate two granola bars. Five minutes into her study, she looked up. "You say you got this from Spence's computer?"

I nodded, taking another bite.

"You know I can't condone what you've done, Ian."

"I know. But I had to."

Bennie burped. "Harboring a fugitive is a felony."

Coach glowered at him. "Is there a point you want to make with that, Ben?"

He stared at her, a silly/serious look on his face. Probably the closest expression to a threat that he could come up with. "It means that you, me, and him are the only ones who know about the school break-in. You pop his cork, I'll pop yours."

"I trust her, Ben. Be quiet," I said.

Coach shook her head. "Ben, you're a good guy, okay? I know you're trying to protect your friend, and I know full well the circumstances we're all in, but being reactionary in a situation like this does no good." She lowered her eyebrows. "And threats don't work on me, so don't ever try it again."

Ben held up his hands, shaking the empty Pepsi can. "Deal. Jesus, Coach, no need to be hard-core about it." He waggled the pop can. "Arm wrestle for another?"

She pointed to the refrigerator. "Help yourself."

I pointed to the list. "What does it mean?"

She sat back, crossing her arms like every other football coach in the world did when they were thinking. "They look like test scores to me," she said, flicking her chin absently with her finger. "How did you do on the WAEE in seventh grade, Ian?"

I thought for a minute. I remembered getting the results that next year. "Not too good. Things were bad then. Why?"

She slid the list to me. "Look at the number by your name. Under the 7 row. Could that be your WAEE test score for the seventh grade?"

"Maybe. I don't remember."

She looked at the list again. "If these are test scores, you did better in the fourth grade than the seventh grade. See?" She handed me the list.

I nodded. "But why is he keeping track of test scores like this?"

She grimaced. "I have an idea of why, but I need time to look into it. Did Principal Spence say anything to you about taking the WAEE this year?"

I shook my head. "No. Ms. Veer did, though. She wanted me to be ready for it."

Coach Schmidt nodded. "I need time, Ian, and that means you need to trust me with this."

"Why?"

"I'm not sure yet, but you need to turn yourself in this morning and wait."

Ben rolled his eyes. "Sort of redundant, Coach. The only thing you do in a cell is wait."

She shot Bennie a look. "Ian, you're on the right track in making things better for yourself and Sammy. See it through."

I looked at her, and knew that I *had* to trust her. "I will."

Ben and I sacked out in his room when we got to his place, and his floor was like the most comfortable bed I'd ever slept in. I was beat. A few hours later, I barely heard Ben get ready for school and leave, and an hour later, I was rubbing the sleep from my eyes and reading a note he'd left me.

> Ian, I'll be there for whatever hearings you have. Good luck, and thanks for setting my shit straight last night.
>
> Ben

Blind Man Thompson was sitting on his porch when I got to his house, and Sammy was inside, watching fuzzy TV on an old black-and-white in the living room. A big tabby cat sprawled itself across his lap, and he was absently petting it, engrossed in the Road Runner outsmarting Wile E. Coyote.

When he saw me, he smiled but didn't get up. I sat next to him on the worn carpet and put my arm around him. "You have a good night, Sam?"

"Sure." He kept his eyes on the TV. "They're gonna come get me now, huh?"

I nodded to the Road Runner, who had just led the poor coyote off a cliff. "Yes."

"You promise Mom'll get better and we can be together?"

"Yes."

"Can you visit me?"

"I don't know," I said. "I will if I can, Sammy."

"I'm sorry I said I didn't want Mom to be our mom anymore. I do."

"That's fine, Sam. I know you do. Things have been tough."

"Will you come with me when they take me?"

I'd thought about this, but I couldn't. They'd arrest me, and I didn't want Sammy to see me cuffed. I didn't want him to think I was anything like the inmates at the penitentiary. I shook my head. "I can't, Sam. I've got to go do my stuff, and you've got to do yours. I'm sorry."

"I understand."

I didn't really think he did understand, but he was being tough. "It'll be all right, bro. I promise." We hugged then, and I kissed him goodbye and walked out. I think it was the hardest thing I'd ever done, and as I said goodbye to Mr. Thompson on the porch, he sensed it, too.

"You come back and visit the blind man when you get straightened up, boy."

I took the phone out. "I don't think we'll ever come back here, Mr. Thompson."

He smiled. "Don't blame you one bit. Good luck."

I walked down the street and dialed the only number I knew to get Sammy taken care of.

"911 emergency. Please state your emergency," the voice said, and I told her where Sammy could be found. She seemed confused until I told her we were runaways, then she said that 911 was for emergencies only. I hung up, figuring he was safer with a blind man than the state and that if they cared enough, they would send somebody out.

I walked for an hour, meandering through the streets and thinking about everything that had happened. It was weird, because I truly had no place to go. Before, when we'd run, we'd been running to something, at least. Now I had nothing to go to but the thing I didn't trust and the thing that didn't care one way or another what happened to us. The system.

I laughed at the thought that the only salvation I could find was in something so screwed up. The courts, cops, judges, counselors, and all the people who made their living shuffling the scum would see me as no different from what they saw every day, and I wondered if they were right. But I also knew from our experience that being alone, hungry, and cold wasn't a dream come true, either. They did what they could, but they couldn't be expected to care. Didn't make me like it any better, but it made me think about it differently.

I took out the cell phone and dialed. "Vice Principal Veer, please."

A moment later, my call was transferred. "Yes?"

"I'm turning myself in."

"Ian?"

"Yes. You said you knew somebody?"

"Yes. Phinias Magnuson. I'll call him right away."

I hung up before she could go on.

A police car, white and blue and with a thick-necked bull sitting behind the wheel holding a radar gun in his hand, idled behind a sign near Second and Wall. I walked up to him. He put the radar gun down as I approached, giving me a practiced cop stare. He glanced at his watch. "Shouldn't you be in school?"

"Not if I'm an outlaw," I said, smiling nervously.

"Don't smart off to me, kid. I'm busy."

"Giving tickets to people trying to make a living?" I shrugged. "I'm turning myself in."

Chapter Twenty-Five

Five hours after small-brained Officer Bernie Moon booked me into the juvenile detention center on assault charges, I was ushered to a conference room. I sat in one of the padded chairs at the table and stared at the empty seats across from me, wondering who would be coming in.

Five minutes later, the door opened behind me, and a short, pudgy man with thin strings of hair combed over his forehead waddled in and sat across from me. About as old as my father, he reminded me of a penguin, and he kept swiping his hair to the side to make sure I didn't see the baldness that everybody but Blind Man Thompson could see. He had a bushy mustache and dark eyes set against a ruddy, rough complexion, and as he set his briefcase on the table and began shuffling papers, I figured this was the beginning of me becoming a case file number and not a person. I wondered how many other case file numbers he had. I also figured, by the look of him, that he was some sort of loser who couldn't get a decent job doing anything else but working with jerk-off kids.

"Are you a lawyer?" I asked.

He busied himself with my file, not raising his eyes but shaking his head. "No." A minute later, he closed his briefcase, set the file in front of him, and stared at me. "My name is Phinias Magnuson, and I'm your counselor. You know Ms. Veer?"

I nodded.

"You are Ian McDermott, and you"—he looked at my file—"have broken the jaw of a teacher at Morrison High School, evaded arrest, been involved in the assault of a police officer, stolen a vehicle, and gotten yourself in a heaping pile of trouble." He looked at me then, studying my face for a moment. "Why did you turn yourself in?"

"Is my brother okay?"

"Answer my question, Ian."

"I'm not going to tell you shit until you tell me how my brother is."

He clasped his hands together on the table. "Okay, here's the deal. I'm your counselor. I need to get into the reasons for everything that's happened so I can represent you in court. If you choose to be difficult with me, you will be hurt by it. Not my choice—yours."

"I'm not being difficult."

"Then answer my question."

We locked eyes. "You heard me."

He leaned back. "I don't know. Your mother turned up in rehab, and that's good, but the state has found clear neglect and child endangerment. That means your brother has been put in receiving care for the time being and will eventually be placed in a foster home for children with fetal drug addiction syndrome. He will remain there until your mother completes a drug-treatment course. A six-month period of observation will follow, then a decision, or long-term plan, will be implemented."

"So in other words, never."

"I don't know, Ian, but I've got you, not your brother."

"I want to talk to him."

He sighed. "Okay. You talk to me, I make arrangements for a call."

I nodded. "Talk, then."

"Tell me why you turned yourself in."

"My brother needs help."

"And you don't?"

"I'm fine, Mr. Magnuson. And I'll do what I need to to get things straight."

"Call me Phinias, and you can stop with the holier-than-thou crap. I know you care about your brother, and that's good, but you didn't turn yourself in just for him, did you?"

I paused. "No."

"Why, then?"

"Because I don't want to be what everybody expects me to be."

"And what is that?"

"A loser. Scumbag. Whatever you see when you look at me."

He smiled, looking at my file. "Did Mr. Florence deserve to have his jaw broken?"

"No."

"Why did you break it, then?"

"I didn't. I hit him and it broke. He must have weak bones. Inbreeding or something."

He didn't take the bait. "Why did you hit him, then?"

I told him the story. How he hated me for not joining the track team, hassled me constantly, and finally grabbed me.

"He touched you first?"

"He swung me around. It was like a reaction. And yes, he did deserve to be hit. Maybe not a broken jaw, but it felt good to do it, and I'd do it again if I had the chance." I looked at him. "Does that make me some kind of psychopath?"

He shook his head. "No. It makes you a teenager with some pretty serious anger issues."

"Tell me about it," I said, deciding I liked the penguin guy across from me.

"Actually, I'd like you to tell *me* about it. All of it."

I did then. I spent an hour telling him about Mom and the drugs, why we ran, the trip to Walla Walla, the meeting with our father, and the trip back. I told him about everything except for Dunbar Phillips and the list. I had to trust Coach Schmidt with the list, and I couldn't trust Phinias yet. And as for Dunbar, I'd sooner be run through the garbage disposal than get him in trouble.

He nodded when I finished, tapping his pen on a pad of paper. "Do you enjoy hitting people?"

"Sometimes. Why does everybody ask that?"

"Because it has much to do with your sentencing, Ian. Patterns and behaviors tell a judge a lot, and if he, or I, think you have a serious problem with violence, it will affect your sentencing and the program guidelines he mandates."

"A propensity for violence."

He nodded. "Exactly. You're a smart kid, so I'll save the sweet talk for the next rich kid with no idea what real problems are. It's all about boundaries, Ian, and how easy you find it to break them. Any good judge isn't going to simply look at the charges in front of him. He'll look at you, at what I say, and at how you conduct yourself."

"What's going to happen?"

"Your father has already hired an attorney for you. I've been in contact with both him and your dad. The school is pushing the charges hard, and you'll be made an example of as a deterrent to school violence. I'm not going to bullshit you about that. It happens, and you're headed for some time spent here. You'll have a hearing if I can't get a mediation session with the school district, the teacher involved, and the district attorney's office. I'm going to try for that, but I've got to tell you right now, they probably won't agree. You've been expelled from ever attending a school in the district, too."

"And after I get out of juvie?"

"Most likely you'll be put into foster care with your brother. Hopefully the same home. The state doesn't like separating siblings. The length of that depends on your mother's ability to complete the program, or your eighteenth birthday—whichever comes first."

"And my dad?"

He slid his eyes to the file, but he wasn't reading anything. "Your father has supplied an attorney and promised to help in any way he finds necessary."

"Any way but living with him, right?"

He nodded. "There hasn't been an offer, but I haven't spoken to him in depth about the issue."

"He's a bastard."

"Maybe he is, Ian, but there are a lot of bastards out there to deal with, and most aren't bastards all the time. You've got to learn to deal with them."

"Deal with them without breaking their jaws, right?" I smirked.

"Right. And your father *is* involved. Sometimes we just have different thresholds for what we can do, and your father is doing what he thinks is best. It's more than others have, if that's any consolation to you."

I left that one alone. "So what happens now?"

"I leave, think about what you've told me, and put my state-paid brilliance to work. I'll push hard for mediation."

I looked at him. "Can I ask you a question, Mr. Magnuson?"

"Shoot."

"Do you like hitting people?"

He smiled. "I believe a more apt question would be 'Do you *wish* you could hit people?' And yes, I do."

"Who?"

He pondered me for a moment. "When I walked in here and saw the way you looked at me when I sat down, you."

I remembered what I'd thought when I saw him. "I'm sorry."

"Don't be. We're all in the same boat for different reasons, Ian." He stood. "Goodbye."

"My phone call?"

He nodded. "Within an hour."

Chapter Twenty-Six

I talked to Sammy from a row of phones set in glass-partitioned cubicles, and I heard other kids laughing and yelling in the background, which made me feel better about where he was. He told me Mrs. Bicelli stayed home all day long and made pancakes and bacon for *dinner*, which was the weirdest thing in the world but tasted good. He also told me he missed me and asked what jail was like. I told him it wasn't that bad. The cells weren't really cells but plain rooms, and I figured if I could deal with Malachi and his boss, I could deal with anybody in here.

All in all, I was surprised at the change in Sammy. He'd been there less than a full day, and he was talking. Not happy, but talking. I told him that Dad had hired an attorney, which he didn't understand, and that Mr. Magnuson was helping me get out as soon as possible.

We spent ten minutes talking before a guard told me time was up, and when I continued talking, he hung the phone up for me, scowling. I ate dinner in the cafeteria, which was the same as at school, but with uniformed guards watching over us. I found a seat away from everybody else and ate alone, thinking about

215

Coach Schmidt and how the list might affect what happened to me.

I hadn't asked Phinias what kind of sentence I might get, and a part of me didn't want to know. From his tone, I was in for it, though. After eating, we had free time for an hour before we were locked down, and I spent it sitting in a chair, pretending I was invisible.

My cellmates were a black guy named Hooper and a white kid, younger than me, named Tory. Tory was in seventh grade and had been busted for stealing his neighbor's car, and Hooper was in for selling a lid of pot to an undercover cop. We talked for a while before the lights went out, and five minutes after that, I was long gone, too, dreaming of running off a cliff and floating away.

Wake-up was six-thirty, and at nine, I had a visitor. I expected Mr. Magnuson, but when I was taken to the visitors' area, my dad sat at a table, his suit and tie looking stiff under the fluorescent lights. He saw me come in the door and gave an awkward wave, making sure I saw him, and I was tempted to turn around and go back.

I sat across from him and shrugged, looking around. "I didn't think you'd show up."

He studied me for a moment. "I know."

I stared at my fingers on the table. "We don't need anything from you."

"You're a strong young man, Ian."

I looked at him, thinking about all the stuff in our lives he hadn't been there for. "Things haven't been easy."

He nodded. "I'm here to try to make things easier for you."

I shook my head. "You're here to make yourself feel better for leaving us."

216

"I'm here to help you."

That pressure in my chest came up again. "Then why is your son in a foster home?"

A flash of anger came to his face, then left just as quickly. "That's not fair, Ian. I—"

The words came in a rush, spilling out like a tidal wave. "Don't talk to me about fair! Sammy needs help, and you know it! He's needed help since he was born, and you've spent the last ten years acting like you don't have two sons, and the worst part about the whole thing is he *knew*. He's not dumb, Dad! He might be slow and have a hard time getting things, but he knew. You sent him back, and he knows the reason! He knows you don't want him and he knows exactly why, and you come in here and say you want to help? How? By pounding it into him that yeah, he has a dad, but he's just not good enough to have him stick around? That we're not good enough for you?" I stood up and wiped my eyes, my face tight with anger. "He spent the whole way down there talking about you! You know that? About how good you must be and that you had to leave after he was born because of a job!" I looked to the ceiling. "A job! Yeah. That's what Mom told him." I brought my eyes to him and saw the pain I was causing, but he needed it. I needed it.

I went on. "I know why you left, and there's nothing you can say to change it. You didn't want us. You didn't want Mom, you didn't want our lives, and you didn't want anything to do with your family. So if you want to come here and try to help any-body, help him, because I can't. Nobody can." I stood staring at him and didn't care if he saw the tears.

He took a breath, slowly letting it out. "I should have seen that coming, and I know I deserve every word of it. But I want to help both of you. Not just your brother. I'm here, Ian, and I'm not going to make any excuses for what I've done. I can't. You deserve the truth. Please. Sit down."

"Just get out."

He didn't move. Didn't speak. Just sat there.

"Go!"

"No." This time his chin trembled just the tiniest bit. "I'm not leaving you until you hear me out. Then I'll do as you ask."

I slumped into the chair. "Then talk."

"I told you that you deserve the truth. I think you know it, but it's important for me to tell you. I left your mother because of the drugs. I couldn't help her. Things were so bad, Ian, and I loved her so much. She almost died twice before Sammy was born, and after a while, I just couldn't stand to look at her. To see what had become of her. So I left. I left before Sammy was born, and I knew he'd be addicted to drugs. A drug baby. I couldn't face it. I couldn't face having a son like that, and I couldn't face what my life had turned into, so I walked out. I left.

"I hated myself for years afterward. I met Sally, and we married. I wrote your mother, sent money, tried to see you, but she wouldn't let me. And I know I didn't try hard enough, either. I could have, Ian, and for that I'm sorry, but there was a part of me that didn't want to. A part that wanted to forget it all. To forget you." He stared at his hands on the table. Big hands just like mine. "I messed up, Ian, and the moment you and Sammy walked into my office, I realized what a tremendous error I had made. I make no excuses. I know I can't change things from how they've been, and I won't ask for your forgiveness, but I'm not leaving you like this. Not again."

I thought about what he said, imagining myself in the same position. Mom hadn't changed, just gotten worse, so I knew

218

what he was saying. I wouldn't have left my kids, though, and that stung. I think it stung deep enough to last a lifetime. But he wanted to help. He wasn't leaving. I stood. "Then help my brother."

"What about you, son?"

I looked at him, and it hurt so bad I thought I'd crumple to the ground and dissolve. "I don't know."

Chapter Twenty-Seven

I went through the motions for the rest of the day, avoiding everybody as best I could, then talked to Sammy for ten minutes just before dinner. He'd spent the day shopping for clothes and was excited; he'd be going back to his usual school the next day, and for that I was happy.

I remembered how he'd do the same thing every day when we got home, looking through the house for Mom, and knew he needed a schedule. Some sort of consistency that maybe I hadn't been able to provide. I wanted to see him and be with him, but as we talked, I started realizing that I'd been right. He needed more than I could give him.

Sammy explained that he'd talked to a woman earlier, before they'd gone shopping, about everything. His counselor, I realized. I told him that was good, and that he should tell her everything he thought about things. He told me he did, also adding that she said I must be a good brother to take care of him like I did. I didn't know how true that was. Then he told me Dad had visited him.

"He did?"

Sammy was excited. "Yeah. We got ice cream."

"Good. What did he say?"

"He asked me about all sorts of stuff. Mom and school and you and what my favorite things to do are. I told him skating with you and playing Clue with Mom. I told him about that stupid-head Elliot who always picks on me, too, and he said he would talk to the principal about it. He said he was going to help, too. Like be here and stuff."

"Good."

"I had chocolate mint."

"That's your favorite, huh?"

"Yep. Two whole scoops. He said I could get ten if I wanted."

At two o'clock the next afternoon, Phinias Magnuson visited, and the first thing he asked me was if I'd been talking to Sammy. I told him that I had, and he nodded, rummaging through his briefcase. Once he had my file in front of him, he clicked a pen absently, staring blankly at the page. Not good news, I assumed.

"Your mother walked out of rehab today, Ian." He raised his pudgy face to me, his comb-over slightly askew. "I'm sorry."

I shrugged. Mom was Mom, and I couldn't change that. "I guess I knew it would happen. Maybe deep down."

"But you were hoping."

"Yeah."

"How do you feel about that?"

"I don't think it matters how I feel about that, Mr. Magnuson."

"Why?"

"Because it just means we do things a different way." I wasn't

221

about to tell him the truth about my mom. I'd spent so long ignoring how much it hurt when she did what she did, I couldn't. Not somebody I hardly knew.

He nodded. "Good. So we will. Sammy is doing well?"

I smiled. "I think so. He's talking, anyway."

He studied me. "What are you afraid of, Ian?"

"That hair, man. You've got to get rid of the old-guy thing."

He shifted. "I know I may be amusing to you, but I'd like to stay on track here."

"What am I afraid of?"

"Yes."

I looked out the window. "I used to be afraid of being a loser my whole life. Like my mom, I guess."

"And now?"

I thought about it for a moment. "I'm afraid I'll be like my dad. That I won't be able to take it anymore."

"Take what?"

"Life. Sammy. Just everything, I guess."

"And your father couldn't take it?"

I shrugged. "He left. It's funny, because I always had it in the back of my mind that he'd be good, you know? That he'd really left because of other reasons."

"And he's not good?"

I remembered what Dad had said about making mistakes, and I believed him. But it didn't change my mind. "No, he's not. Or he wasn't, anyway." I looked at Phinias. "He did leave because of us, you know? But he also left because of him. Of the way he is."

"What does that make him?"

"I don't know. But it makes me mad."

"Justifiably so, I think," Phinias said. "But he's trying to make up for it now, isn't he?"

"Sort of. In the only way he can, I guess." I thought about it for a second. "It's funny, because he's everything I'd probably wish our dad would be, but then I realized he's everything I hate, too."

He nodded. "Like you said, Ian, you and your father are different people. You're working hard not to be like him, aren't you? Or at least that part of him?"

"I'm not skating out on everything, am I?"

He smiled. "No. Just lay off on the fists, and we'll be fine."

We talked for a few more minutes, and it was interesting. Phinias talked about accepting people for what they were and moving on, and I was reminded of what I'd said to Bennie about his dad. Maybe I should, and maybe just like Ben, I wasn't ready to. He also talked to me about working within the system to get what I need instead of busting out of it all the time. Fighting the system was fine, he said, but fighting it the right way was the key.

Phinias told me my lawyer would be visiting the next day with a hearing date, and that though they'd both been pushing for a mediation hearing, the district attorney's office, urged by the school district, wouldn't budge. I'd be burned at the stake as if I were a witch, I thought, and it sucked big-time.

The next day came and went, with no lawyer showing up. Life "on the inside" wasn't that bad, and I didn't have any real trouble, just attitude from a few bullies that a hard stare or two had taken care of. I talked to Sammy. His day at school had gone well, and we spent the rest of our ten minutes talking about his homework. Dad had called the principal and talked to her about Elliot.

Just before dinner, my lawyer, Neil Mazuto, showed up. He

looked fresh off the rack, clean-cut, abrupt, and in a hurry. I asked him when my hearing was, and he told me I wouldn't be having one. He shook his head like something had happened that he didn't know about. "They did a one-eighty on the mediation hearing. In fact, the superintendent of the school district demanded it." He crossed his leg over his knee and leaned back, steepling his fingers. "Word has it he's ruffled quite a few feathers in going against Morrison High's administration. They don't like you one bit, Mr. McDermott."

"The feeling is mutual. When is the mediation?"

"Tomorrow. It also means that if we're successful, you won't have a sentencing hearing for the assault on the teacher. Possibly community service, a short stay in juvenile, or a restriction on your activity if things go well for us. I've talked with your counselor, Mr. Magnuson, and he has explained the circumstances of the assault. Coach Florence touched you first?"

"Yes."

He nodded, taking up a pen and scribbling. "As far as the assault on the sheriff, those charges have been dropped and you've been assigned probationary status, which means you'll have to report in weekly and keep your nose clean until you're eighteen. You can thank your father for that, and also for talking to the owner of the truck. They're not pressing charges."

I sat, remembering what Jacob had said about making things right with the sheriff. "I'll need to talk to the sheriff."

He shrugged it off. "Your choice, and something that you can do later." He fingered some papers. "Now, as for the whole episode with the two guards at the rest stop, I'm thinking the DA won't pursue it. You weren't officially detained. If we can't do that, the charge will stand alone and you'll be sentenced, though your father is again whispering in the court's ear. He's a powerful man, so I'm thinking it will in fact be included in the mediation hearing."

"Where is he?"

"Your father?"

I nodded.

"He was called back to Walla Walla on business."

I let that one drop. "Tomorrow, then?"

He picked up his case. "See you then."

Chapter Twenty-Eight

*T*he mediation session was scheduled for ten in the morning, and as I was transported, along with four other guys, to the courthouse, I wondered what would happen.

When we arrived, Phinias stood by the curb waiting for me. He'd gotten his hair cut. The wisps were gone. He smiled and nodded. "This mediation is the best thing we could have hoped for, Ian."

We walked up the stairs and into the building. "Where do I go if I get out?"

"Didn't your attorney tell you?"

"No. What?"

"After the mediation and whatever is decided there, you'll most likely have a hearing with"—he looked at a slip of paper—"Judge Tompkins. He'll make a final judgment and mandate a sentence for the other charge of fleeing; probation, community service, or some other restriction would be my guess, depending on his mood. And that's only if the DA wants to pursue it."

We reached a long hall, and three doors down on the right,

we entered a room with a conference table set in the middle. On the far side of the table sat Principal Spence, Vice Principal Veer, Coach Florence with his jaw wired shut, and one other man, an outright enormous guy in a huge blue suit, his jowls flowing over his collar. At the end of the table sat a woman in a green blazer with a typing machine in front of her.

Across from them sat my attorney, Mr. Mazuto. To his right was my father. He nodded to me as I entered. I'd wondered if he would be here and was surprised. Phinias showed me to a chair next to my attorney, then took a seat next to me. "Gentlemen and lady." He nodded.

Greetings were made around the table, and when Phinias introduced Samuel McDermott as my father, Principal Spence and Coach Florence raised their eyebrows. Vice Principal Veer stood, a sincere smile on her face, and stretched her arm over the table. "Mr. McDermott. Very nice to meet you."

My father left his chair, towering over the table. He took her hand. "Nice to meet you, too, ma'am." As he sat down, he shot a glance to Principal Spence, who returned it with a certain amount of contempt scrawled across his face.

The huge guy turned out to be from the district attorney's office. Tate Indy was his name. Mr. Indy gave me a swipe with his eyes, then opened a folder. Ms. Veer, Spence, and Coach Florence were somber, with Spence fidgeting impatiently.

Indy began. "We've agreed to this mediation session because Mr. Hopkins, the district superintendent, requested it. Neither the district attorney's office, the victim, nor the administration of Morrison High School is in agreement with this, but at the request of Mr. Hopkins, mediation has been accepted."

Phinias smiled. "That collar around your neck a bit tight today, Tate?"

Tate smiled. "Just a bit." He nodded to Phinias's haircut. "Nice to see you've joined the twenty-first century."

Phinias glanced my way and smiled. "Every dog has his day, Tate. Are we ready?"

Principal Spence leaned forward, folding his hands together and pointing to me like his fingers were a laser pistol. "This young man brutally assaulted one of my teachers, and regardless of the superintendent's wishes for a mediation hearing, I cannot allow this to happen at my school or allow lenience in the handing down of punishment for it."

My attorney, Mr. Mazuto, drummed his fingers on the table, waiting for Spence to finish. "With all due respect, Mr. Spence, your authority to administer punishment ends at the exit doors of your school. This is a mediation, not a dictatorship. Mr. McDermott is here to face the charges brought against him, and is willing to mediate a compromise to those charges and resolve this in a manner beneficial to all."

Principal Spence jabbed his finger at me, his eyes flicking to my dad before he went on. "He's dangerous. To the community and the school. And while Vice Principal Veer, myself, and several other teachers tried to help Mr. McDermott, he rejected that help out of hand, alluding to 'shooting up' the school on one occasion." He glanced at Ms. Veer for support, but she remained still. "In addition, he has threatened another coach previous to attacking Mr. Florence."

My father cut in, his voice deep and soft, but commanding. His eyes were riveted on Principal Spence. "My son has made mistakes. He is in violation of the law. This mediation hearing is assembled today for those actions to be discussed, the consequences of those actions to be dealt with, and punishment to be handed down." He rose and stepped away from his chair. "This mediation hearing is also to be utilized in a way beneficial to the future of this young man. This is not a witch hunt. This is not a trial." His eyes blazed into Spence. "This, sir, is not an arena for personal vendetta, slander, or exaggeration." He set his big knuckles on the table, leaning his bulk toward Principal Spence. "Are we clear, sir?"

Spence shifted back in his chair, but his eyes stayed on my dad. "The boy is dangerous."

My father stayed put. "Do you know what the legal definition is of an individual considered dangerous to the community, sir?"

Spence hesitated. He didn't know what my father did for a living. "Well, I think Ian has proven himself to be dangerous to the community." He gestured to Coach Florence. "I don't think a normal person would do this."

My father lowered his voice, and I knew Spence had pushed the wrong buttons with him. "I'm not asking you what you think, sir. I'm asking you what you *know.*"

Principal Spence leveled flinty eyes, the challenge well met. He was pissed. Then Phinias scribbled on a piece of scrap paper, giving a smug smile as my eyes went to it. It read: *You are speaking to the chief administrator of the Washington State Penitentiary.* Phinias slid the paper to Principal Spence. Spence read it, and the look on his face changed. If anybody in the room had experience with dangerous individuals, it was my dad. "I wasn't aware that you were the superintendent of the state penitentiary."

My father's eyes lingered on him for a moment, dismissing the comment with the indifference of an elephant swatting a fly. He addressed the room. "What we *know* is that Ian has broken the law. He has assaulted a teacher. He ran. Not to escape punishment, but to help his brother. He returned of his own free will to face the charges brought against him. This in itself shows my son is aware of his actions and willing to submit to the law. He has shown youthful indiscretion and poor decision-making skills, but his actions were clearly not born of malice. Only of desperation and frustration, coupled with an inability to act in a mature fashion. Considering the events and hardships in his life leading up to the assault and following circumstances, his reactions, though not in any way justified, are understandable. In essence, Ian has shown exactly what he is. A troubled youth with an anger-management problem." He paused. "In addition, he has shown himself to be a young man with the skills and motivations to conquer those troubles, as his presence in this room indicates." With that, he sat down. Silence filled the room. He folded his hands on the table, then looked to District Attorney Indy. "Please continue."

I'd never seen a guy get the shit kicked out of him without a punch being landed, but there's a first time for everything, and my father had shown how to do it. Principal Spence offered nothing in return.

Tate Indy nodded. "Principal Spence, you claim threats were made by Mr. McDermott?"

"Yes."

My attorney, Mr. Mazuto, cut in. "Were any punishments handed down or charges filed against Mr. McDermott for these alleged threats, Mr. Spence?" Mazuto looked at my school file. "I'm not seeing any corrective action having taken place."

Principal Spence grimaced. "In the hopes of counseling Mr. McDermott, I declined pressing charges for the incident with Coach Schmidt." His eyes flickered to my father. "I was hoping to help the young man, and perhaps I made an error of judgment in not pursuing legal recourse."

Mr. Mazuto nodded, looking to the DA. "These allegations have no place in this mediation hearing."

Principal Spence went on, his tone more officious. "I know you may not understand my position, Mr. Mazuto, but I am responsible for not just one but over fifteen hundred students. Their safety and well-being is my priority."

Phinias smiled bitterly. "But your responsibility seemed not to lie, in many ways, with Mr. McDermott. I see no notes attached concerning counseling recommendations, corrective action plans, or . . . well, anything besides one three-day suspension and five days of detention. Other than pushing him out of your school, I see no action having been taken to help Ian. " He narrowed his eyes at Principal Spence. "Would you mind taking a minute to explain that, Mr. Spence?" He turned his gaze to Ms. Veer. "Or you, Ms. Veer?"

I knew something was going on, and I had a feeling Phinias was the only one in the room who knew what it was. Principal Spence shifted in his seat. "I was not pushing him out. I was convinced that the trouble Ian was having at Morrison could be remedied at Kerner Alternative. In my judgment, he would have been better served there. What does this have to do with assaulting a teacher?"

Mr. Mazuto turned to Phinias, raising his eyebrows. Phinias smiled. "Why, nothing, Mr. Spence, but perhaps some light needs to be shed on why Mr. McDermott was placed in a situation where he felt pressure to leave."

Principal Spence exhaled, thinking for a moment. "He was not pressured. He was counseled. By Vice Principal Veer and myself."

Phinias tapped his finger on the table. "Did you inform Ian that you could *guarantee* his tenure at Morrison High wouldn't be beneficial, and that you were *cleaning up this school*? In what manner were you cleaning up Morrison High School?"

231

Spence looked at me. "I don't recall saying it that way, sir. I do recall advising Mr. McDermott that his stay at Morrison High might not be as beneficial as transferring to an alternative school."

Phinias smiled, looking to his notes. "Because of his *aptitude?*"

Ms. Veer looked to Principal Spence. "You told him that?"

"I certainly did not."

Tate Indy interjected. "Phinias—"

Phinias doodled on his notepad. "It will become apparent, I believe, that Mr. McDermott's aptitude does indeed have something to do with this mediation hearing."

I knew then what it was. *The list.*

Principal Spence clenched his teeth, then turned to the DA. "Let's proceed with the mediation."

The DA, confused by the turn the conversation had taken, shook his head. "As Mr. McDermott noted, Ian had no justification for assaulting Mr. Florence. He—"

Just then, somebody knocked on the door. Phinias smiled, rising from his seat.

The DA furrowed his brow. "This is a closed mediation session, Phinias. . . ."

When he opened the door, an older man with a stack of files walked in. Principal Spence, Vice Principal Veer, and Coach Florence suddenly came to attention, straightening their backs and nodding to the man. Spence's eyes flicked to Phinias.

The man nodded to the gathering and sat at the head of the table, opposite the typist, who had been recording the session.

Phinias sat back down. "Gentlemen and lady, I'm sure you know, but this is Mr. Hopkins, superintendent of District 9."

Greetings and mumblings were made, and Mr. Hopkins, an older man with no tie, his top button undone, and sharp, piercing

232

eyes, tapped the folders in front of him. "I apologize for being late. I've had much work to do since yesterday and found myself running behind." He smiled at me. "I'm tardy, it seems."

The DA sat back, glancing at Phinias before speaking to Superintendent Hopkins. "Well, it seems I'm unaware of certain circumstances here, Superintendent Hopkins. You're here to enlighten us with something?"

The superintendent leveled a stare at Principal Spence. "Indeed I am, sir."

Principal Spence fidgeted. "Sir, with all due respect—"

The superintendent cut in. "Mr. Spence, please remain silent." He opened the first file. "I was contacted yesterday afternoon by a person concerned with Mr. McDermott's circumstances, and this person alluded to the fact that Mr. McDermott has been unfairly targeted by certain key individuals at Morrison High School. This disturbed me. I was then furnished with these files." He tapped the stack. "Upon inspection, I found that Mr. McDermott, along with several dozen of his classmates, has been put on *a list.*" He lowered his brows at Principal Spence. "A list compiled by you, sir."

Principal Spence's face went white. "I don't know what you are talking about. Surely I do keep files of students who are having trouble at Morrison, but to say . . ."

The superintendent stared at him. "What am I saying?"

Spence shut his mouth.

Hopkins went on, looking to the DA. "These are the files of the students found on the list kept by Mr. Spence. I was told to correlate the seventh-grade WAEE scores of those students to the rest of the student body, compare the results, look up the status of enrollment of said students and their subgroups, and find a pattern. The pattern became clear." He stared at Spence. "Under state and federal guidelines, students are expected to achieve certain test scores or they do not graduate high school with proper documentation. In addition, those scores dictate budget allowances for individual schools, and poor scores would necessitate improvement plans, which cost the school, and district, extra money. Money that would come from the general budget of the school."

He didn't take his eyes from Principal Spence. "WAEE is administered in the fourth, seventh, tenth, and twelfth grades, with testing slated for all grades in the future." Mr. Hopkins went on as the DA's face tightened. "As you can imagine, the status and respect of a school is highly dependent on those scores. In simple terms, if a school is mandated to spend more of its budget on helping students pass the WAEE, that money has to be taken from other programs such as . . . sports." He riveted his eyes on Principal Spence. "In those terms, it should be a motivation for administrations to serve the student body in a way to *educate* those high-risk students to achieve success, not push out those who don't fit in with your vision."

Spence remained silent.

The DA shook his head. "Superintendent Hopkins, are you saying that Morrison High School is expelling students who didn't score well on the seventh-grade WAEE?"

"More than that. We have guidelines in place to inhibit the overall number of expulsions at a school. What this list implies is that students who did not score well in the seventh grade and who then come to Morrison High School more often than not are *pushed* out before they take the tenth-grade test." Superintendent Hopkins stared daggers at Principal Spence. "There are striking disparities in both expulsion and transfer rates."

The DA gave Superintendent Hopkins a wondering look.

Hopkins went on. "The district keeps track of total expulsions for each school, but the reasons why, though documented, are not included in the summaries." He raised his eyes to Principal Spence. "In essence, the criteria for expulsion at your school are lopsided. Some students have been expelled while others have not been, and though it may be a case of poor judgment and incompetence on your part, Mr. Spence, I do see a pattern." He paused. "WAEE scores."

Principal Spence drew himself up. "I—"

Superintendent Hopkins cut him off. "That does not concern me as I sit in this room, though it will soon. Mr. McDermott has not been expelled as of yet, but he has indeed been targeted. The students on that list have been *pressured*. Not to pass the tests but to move to different schools such as Kerner Alternative. In the last two years, twenty-seven of those students have enrolled in different schools, and eight of those are now dropouts." He passed a graph to Indy. "I've graphed the rates. Morrison High School has had an enormous transfer and dropout rate in the three months prior to the tenth-grade WAEE test for the last three years, which happens to fall right in line with Mr. McDermott's being asked to leave one month before the testing. This is disparate and worthy of investigation."

Principal Spence clenched his teeth. "Morrison High's dropout and expulsion rates are right in line with those of the other high schools in this district, and certainly within the guidelines. How can you say—"

Superintendent Hopkins held up his hand for silence. "I do not have an issue with the rates, sir. I have an issue with *who* those students are, *why* they are chosen, and why there seems to be an enormous jump in those students leaving Morrison High in the months before the WAEE. It is clear to me from the list you compiled and the data I have studied that Morrison High School is playing a game with the lives of young people."

Phinias tapped his finger on the table. "Didn't the districting change four years ago?"

Mr. Hopkins nodded. "It did. My tenure here has included the melding of diverse neighborhoods in hopes of bringing understanding and a level playing field to the learning process. It seems that Principal Spence, and possibly Vice Principal Veer, used that as a motivating factor in creating this list."

Vice Principal Veer's eyes had been widening. With Superintendent Hopkins's statement that she might be involved, she took a deep breath, then exhaled, addressing the superintendent. "I understand your suspicions concerning me, Superintendent Hopkins, and I find them absolutely justified." She paused. "I came to Morrison High three years ago, as you must know. It has been my first position as a vice principal." She looked down. "I'm shocked, but I shouldn't be surprised." Her tone softened. "I realized with Ian that my job at Morrison High School is not simply to follow the rules, and while I may look guilty, I must say that any complicity or aid I may have given to such a policy has been given not because I knew of it but because I have been blind to the political side of my position." Spence fidgeted as Ms. Veer went on. "I may well have been used to further an agenda I find horrifying, and as your investigation unfolds, I have no doubt in my mind that the only guilt belonging to me is ignorance. I apologize sincerely and will resign if asked."

Superintendent Hopkins nodded. "Thank you. And I thank you for your understanding of my position. This will be investigated, and you will be investigated along with the entire faculty and administration of Morrison High. If things are as you say, you've no need to fear for your job."

Vice Principal Veer's eyes came up to meet his. "Though I am concerned about my job, right now I'm concerned about those students, including Ian, who have not been served well at Morrison."

Principal Spence's face regained some color. Too much color. "This is ridiculous. I would never compromise any student in a way denoting racism, bias, or past test scores, and that list doesn't prove anything. I simply was targeting those students who needed help in passing the tests."

Superintendent Hopkins threw him another chart. "Would you care to explain how ninety percent of all transfers and expulsions at your school happen in the months previous to the tenth- and twelfth-grade testing period? Would you care to explain why, of that ninety percent, eighty-seven percent of those transferred students had failed the WAEE in the seventh grade."

Spence sputtered. "It is coincidence. Nothing more. Students who do not do well on the WAEE usually exhibit behavioral problems. It is a fact that many would do better at a vocational school. Surely you could see that, sir."

Superintendent Hopkins shook his head. "I've correlated the four other district high schools' records against Morrison High's, Principal Spence. It is not coincidence, and until a full investigation has been completed, you are no longer principal of Morrison High School. You are on administrative leave until the investigation is complete. But if you do in fact care for our school district, a tendered resignation would be fitting, as I don't see you being happy working under my leadership." He glanced at me. "In fact, Principal Spence, I can *guarantee* you won't."

Spence was flustered. "You can't do this. There's no proof."

Superintendent Hopkins slid a paper across the table. "Is this familiar to you, sir?"

Spence gaped.

Superintendent Hopkins went on. "It's a memo of implication. From you to a certain office employee who is right now talking to a team of investigators about this scheme." As Superintendent Hopkins finished, I could only stare at him. The way I understood it, *his* district would benefit from what Spence had done, but here he was, raking Spence over the coals. Silence filled the conference room, and I didn't know what would happen next.

"So," I said, "what happens with the mediation hearing?"

Superintendent Hopkins looked to Indy. "I will be taking the place of Principal Spence as the representative of Morrison High School for the remainder of the mediation." He looked to Spence. "You are free to go."

Principal Spence stood, indignant and stiff, and walked out. There was nothing left for him to say.

Once he was gone, Phinias smiled and clicked open his phone. "I don't think it would be appropriate for this mediation hearing to go forward without Ian's guardian present." His eyes twinkled when he looked at me, then he dialed his phone. A mumbled word or two later, the door opened. Coach Schmidt walked in wearing a pair of slacks and a blouse. I'd never seen her in anything other than sweats.

She nodded, then sat down next to Phinias. "Hello."

I looked past Phinias to her, confused. Phinias looked to my father. "Mr. McDermott?"

He cleared his throat. "In the hopes that Ian will come to accept an invitation to live with me, I have granted guardianship, at her request, to Ms. Schmidt." He turned to me. "I'm taking your brother home, Ian. To my home. And you are welcome at any time."

I was dumbstruck. "What . . ."

He nodded. "Do you feel comfortable with this? I will be making arrangements for you to visit any time you'd like, and if you decide it is not in your best interests to live in Walla Walla, that is your choice. But be assured Sammy will be taken care of."

I looked at him. He didn't have a smile on his face, but I could see it in his eyes. He was proving himself. He was sincere. "Th-that's fine," I stammered. Sammy would get help. I didn't know if I could ever live with my father, but now I knew I could if I wanted to. "What about Mom?"

"We'll keep trying." His eyes pierced mine for a long moment, full of more truth than any words could express. He turned to Tate Indy. "Shall we proceed?"

District Attorney Indy cleared his throat. "Principal Spence and Coach Florence have requested Ian be banned from attending high school in District 9 for the remainder of his education. In addition, the assault charges will be upheld, with three months in juvenile detention mandated, along with probation." He looked at Coach Florence. "With the severity of the injury taken into consideration, I agreed before this meeting to bring this request to the table. Coach Florence?"

Coach Florence took a breath, then cleared his throat. His jaw was wired shut, and he spoke through his teeth. "When Principal Spence spoke to me about Ian, I thought it was with the best of intentions," he mumbled through his wires. "I may be considered a harsh teacher at Morrison, but what happened here is wrong, and it sickens me to think that I've been an unwitting participant in this ordeal." He looked at me. "I cannot condone what happened in the gymnasium, Mr. McDermott, but neither can I condone what might have brought you to feeling like you had no other alternative but to lash out." He looked at Indy, then Hopkins. "I will drop the charges under the condition that Ian's expulsion from the district remain intact. I think that under the circumstances, this is a fair compromise. He should not be allowed attendance after assaulting a teacher." He looked at me then. "I would also request an apology."

I thought of how much I'd hated him, and how that could change so quickly. He might still be a bastard, but I knew I shouldn't have hit him. "I'm sorry."

Indy sat back, throwing his pen on his files and smirking at Phinias. "This is the screwiest mediation I've ever attended, Phinias, but I guess I shouldn't be surprised, with you involved."

Phinias laughed. "Well, my friend, the work of the underdog can never be ignored." He patted my shoulder. "This young man has potential, and I would ask you to see it when recommending sentencing for fleeing the prison transport."

Indy studied me. "He wasn't technically arrested, but he was detained by a law enforcement official." He nodded to my father, who nodded back. "I'll go for one year probation, state-mandated anger-management counseling, a grade point average of three for one year, and one hundred hours' community service." He addressed the superintendent. "Sir?"

He looked at me. "Reasonable. I agree."

Phinias looked at me, then my attorney, then my father, who nodded. "Deal."

As we shuffled out, Superintendent Hopkins turned to me. "Best of luck, Mr. McDermott. You have my apologies for what has happened here, and I would hope"—he gave me a stern look—"that it has taught you that the law can help you as much as it can punish you."

"It has." I paused, thinking about what had happened. He was right. "Thank you."

As the room emptied, I met Vice Principal Veer at the door. From the clouds in her eyes, I could tell she was still upset about the list. I smiled. "I have something for you."

She hesitated, wondering what I was talking about.

I took her cell phone from my pocket and handed it to her. "I'll pay the bill."

She took the phone, and her chin quivered. "I'm sorry this happened, Ian. You'll never know how sorry."

I smiled. "Not your fault. Mine. Thank you." I hugged her then. She'd kept her word to me, and when I didn't believe her, it hadn't mattered to her. "Bye."

After she'd gone, Coach Schmidt shook my dad's hand. "Nice to finally meet you in person, sir."

He smiled. "Call me Sam. And it's nice to meet you, too. I'm sure we'll be getting to know each other better."

"I'm sure we will." She gave me a sidelong glance. "I do have rules, young man. I hope you know what you're getting yourself into here."

I smiled. "No worries."

She looked at Phinias and cocked her head toward the door. "Care for some lunch, Mr. Magnuson? I'm buying."

He smiled. "I'm game for anything free that fills my stomach." He turned to my dad. "Mr. McDermott, it's been a pleasure."

Dad shook his hand. "Likewise, counselor."

Then they were gone, and it was just me and Dad. We faced each other in the empty room, him in his suit and tie and me in a T-shirt I'd worn for over a week, and the distance of our differences shrank under the weight of what had happened. A part of me still looked at him and thought it would all fall apart, but another part of me had to believe it wouldn't. Sammy would have a good home, and I'd get through this. I ached thinking about my bro and me being apart, even for a short while, but I didn't know if I could ever bring myself through his front door. There was also Mom. She needed somebody. "I guess this is where I say thanks."

He shook his head, and I saw something in his eyes that meant more than anything else. Respect. He smiled, holding the door open for me. "This is where we go get your brother."

Acknowledgments

My writing exists today because of three people.
My wife of fifteen years, Kimberly, helped me beat the odds.
Thomas Dudley, my cousin and friend, always believed.
Chris Crutcher, my mentor, taught me that the best teachers are
the teachers who believe not only in what they teach,
but in who they teach.

Thanks to my mother and father, who survived the teenage
years of a kid who simply didn't fit in to the educational system.
My thanks also go to my brothers, Robert and Jason. The bond
of brotherhood portrayed in this story rings true because of
them. I would like to thank George Nicholson of Sterling Lord
Literistic, my agent, for his sincerity, experience, passion, and
belief in a guy like me. Joan Slattery and Allison Wortche, my
editors and guides, thank you. I would also like to thank a
timeless place called The River.

To Stormy and Carol Bruckner, Jhon Goodwin, Toni Foster,
Adam Foster, Chris and Ingrid Batt, Bill and Suzy Smith, Mary
Haworth, and Carol Thomas, my readers, advisors, loved ones,
and friends, thank you. And yes, for the patience they showed
at the table in the back room where thousands of pages have
been written, my gratitude goes to Cheryl, Ronda, Rose,
Shannon, Yvonne, Denisa, and my advisor on all things female,
Donna.

ALSO BY MICHAEL HARMON

The Last Exit to Normal

When Ben Campbell was fourteen years old, his father made an announcement. He called it coming out. Ben called it selfishly blowing apart the family without stopping to think about anyone else.

Three years, countless joints, and one arrest later, Ben finds himself yanked out of his city life and plunked down in eastern Montana with his father and Edward, the Boyfriend. As if arriving in a hicksville town with hair spikes, a skateboard habit, and two dads isn't painful enough, Ben soon realizes something is gravely wrong at the house next door.

Eleven-year-old Billy is guarding a secret about his family, and Ben is determined to set things right. Under that bright and unforgiving Montana sky, Ben's search for the truth reveals an unexpected malice in the sleepy little town—and a situation much more tangled than he could have imagined.

In an authentic, unaffected, and mordantly funny voice, acclaimed author Michael Harmon tells the wrenching story of an uprooted and uncomfortable teenage guy struggling to fix the broken lives around him—while coming to terms with his own.